MUSCLES, MUSIC AND MURDER

A Buckeye Barrister Mystery

by

David M. Selcer

For information, email **Cozy Cat Press**,

cozycatpress@aol.com   or   visit   our   website at:www.cozycatpress.com

COZY CAT
P R E S S

ISBN: 978-1-939816-28-3

Printed in the United States of America

Cover design by Nicole

http://www.covershotcreations.com

1 2 3 4 5 6 7 8 9 10

For Evie

CHAPTER ONE

It was opening night, the first concert of the season, and my friend Rosanne Harmon and I had splurged for tickets—fifth row center—because she loves going to the symphony. We were sitting in The Ohio Theater, previously a posh gilded movie house and performance hall with great acoustics, built in 1918. It had become the home of the Columbus Symphony Orchestra in the 1970s.

Tonight it was ablaze with lights and rigged with four brass cannons to shoot blanks for the climactic volley of cannon fire, ringing chimes and brass fanfare that is the finale of Tchaikovsky's *1812 Overture*. Having suffered a players' strike the previous season, nobody could be sure if the orchestra still had a following, and it was hoped that a piece as large as the *1812 Overture* would bring concert-goers back.

Not to worry, the notables of the city's aristocracy—CEOs, state legislators, the Mayor, and every member of the Columbus Symphony Board, the most revered non-profit organization in the community—were all in attendance. There were also public figures from the music world, including the orchestra's former director, Janic Vadea, who was accompanied by Barbara Gamon, the *Columbus Dispatch* music critic. Most important, there was an overflowing crowd of just plain ordinary classical music lovers.

Rosanne and I passed Symphony Board President Heinrich Wabstmann on our way into the building, where he was busy holding court in the lobby at one of the champagne bars. He was scoffing at the orchestra's newly hired maestro, whom the Board had selected over his negative vote. "This guy better be good. I wouldn't care if we shipped him straight back to Siberia, where he came from," the rich little German-born mogul whined.

"More likely, he'd be headed for Vienna, Budapest or St. Petersburg, Russia if he left here, Hank. That's where the really big European symphonies hang out." Art Malone, one of the symphony trustees, was speaking as he put his arm around Wabstmann's shoulder.

Wabstmann shuddered. Being called "Hank" by Malone was obviously unacceptable. Malone, an eccentric trustee on the symphony Board was wearing his usual snakeskin boots, with wide carved leather belt, a turquoise blue shirt and a string tie with no jacket. He was my only multi-millionaire client. He used me as his sole collection lawyer in central Ohio.

I'm Winston Barchrist III, and all of these people are way above my station in life. When I lost my position as a corporate lawyer at one of Chicago's huge firms, I came to Columbus to pick up the pieces and started a career as a single practitioner doing simple divorces and defending small time thugs. I could hardly afford the price of a fifth row center seat tonight. But I did it for Rosanne—my girl. She bought her ticket and I bought mine.

The concert was about to begin as we reached our seats. The lights went low. A large bald-headed man dressed in formal tails ascended the podium to tentative applause that gradually became thunderous. He was Igor Bashenko, the symphony's new conductor. As the orchestra moved into the strains of the overture to Mozart's 15th, we adjusted ourselves in our seats. The crowd loved it. Three short Strauss waltzes followed, which they also ate up.

After intermission, came a more modernistic work entitled *Pictures at an Exhibition* by Mussorgsky, along with some church pieces composed by Vivaldi, and then, finally, Tchaikovsky's *1812 Symphony Overture.* The maestro soared through this 19th Century piece as the long wavy white hair fringing his bald scalp danced around his head. When Tchaikovsky's bold final stanzas began to build, he urged on the brass section. He cued the chimes and encouraged the strings toward their finale. And then, the cannons went off and the timpani drums rolled, again... and again, electrifying the audience, as the final crescendos began.

Suddenly, during a pause in the music, I heard a clink, and something ricocheted off a music stand. Just before the overture boomed to its conclusion in a hail of bravos and applause, I heard two more metallic clanks.

The entire audience was on its heels. Bashenko began to turn toward the crowd to bow, but there was something, something different. He faltered. Blood was spreading slowly across his formal white shirt from under his waistcoat. The concertmaster, awaiting the maestro's customary acknowledgement of her, looked up at him and screamed.

"Get an ambulance!" someone yelled as Bashenko's knees buckled and he fell off the podium crashing to the floor. The symphony players closed in around him, their tuxedos forming a black curtain. The maestro was close to death, but not there yet.

CHAPTER TWO: THREE MONTHS EARLIER

Dick Wasserberg's neighborhood saloon on the South side still had the original mahogany bar in it from 1931, and the highly seasoned brats and warm, buttered sauerkraut his grandfather invented were still being served. There were photographs of every Columbus mayor for the last 80 years on the walls, all shaking hands with one or another member of the Wasserberg family. The only thing that had changed was the neighborhood. Looking at Wass's from the outside, you expected to meet only low class clientele inside, but instead it was a place where you met the same people every time—elderly patrons, grandchildren of former patrons now deceased, the luncheon crowd from the nearby courthouse community, beat cops and bikers...all very middle class.

"How about a St. Pauli's Girl?" Wass asked, sliding one down the bar at me, which he always did when I walked in. He was dressed in his OSU sweatshirt from the Official Online Store of the Big Ten Conference with a scarlet and grey cap on his head. It was time for "March Madness," and to Wass, March Madness was more than just the premier college basketball tournament of the year, more than just another reason to create an office betting pool. It was something to be observed annually like Lent, especially this year since OSU was doing so well.

"Yah, thanks, Wass. Why not?" Which was what I always said when he slid one at me. How he never managed to spill any of the beer when he did this was beyond me. I was on my way home from my law office, which is over the Dairy Mart at 108 Whittier Avenue just across the street from Plank's restaurant and bar in Columbus. It's on the edge of the old German Village area, the rough edge, not the quaint part filled with newly tuck-pointed Nineteenth Century refurbished brick houses, swank stores and sophisticated little insurance and attorneys offices.

I glanced up at the television. The local news was reporting a murder over at the Arnold Schwarzenegger Fitness Classic. The Fitness Classic is a body-building event Schwarzenegger holds each year at Veteran's Memorial here in Columbus. I don't think Arnold really runs it, especially now that he's the governor of California. He just appears there to fulfill his endorsement contracts with exercise machine manufacturers and various sports retailers. It's an annual pro-am event. Anyway, the reporter was announcing that they found a dead body builder inside one of the spray booths during the amateur competition.

"Jeez, there's a real waste of some prime beefcake," Trudy Fischel rasped as she sidled up and planted her barely-covered derriere on the stool next to me. "Wonder what his name was."

Trudy is a computer geek, actually an accomplished computer hacker, from New York with an investigator's license, whom I sometimes employ to help me with some of my cases. In her mid-forties, she has long bleached blond hair and nice legs, although she's beginning to look a lot like the women who advertise on Cheaters.com

"What's a spray booth anyways?" I asked.

"Oh, that! That's like a tanning booth where a body builder goes inside and gets sprayed down with special oils while he's tanning, to make his body glisten in the competition while he's up on the stage flexing. I used to do it myself when I competed in bikini competitions."

"You competed in—"

"It was a while ago, boss. Now don't get all starchy on me."

"—a bikini—"

"—yah, back in the day, I guess I was something to behold."

"—contest?"

"Well, at least it was exciting. What do you do for excitement, Winston? Eat Hershey Bars on the couch and watch basketball? Look at how heavy you are. You weigh over 300 pounds. At least I competed in something besides a fat man's contest."

Trudy could cut you to the core if she wanted, and apparently this time she wanted to. I don't know what I said that was wrong, but I don't think I deserved that. I watched her retreat outside to smoke. If there weren't a lot of patrons in the place Wass would let her smoke inside, even though it was against the law. But today there were too many people around.

Suddenly, the TV above the bar caught my attention again. This time, it was a shot of a black limousine pulling away from the airport.

"And, in other news, the orchestra's new maestro skipped his Columbus debut today," the announcer's voice was saying as the scene of an empty black limousine slowly vanished down the airport road. The teaser caught my attention because the new director of the Columbus Symphony Orchestra was the father of one of my clients. I decided to wait through the advertisements until the news came back on, and they ran the story.

"Something tells me that man doesn't belong here," Wass offered, glancing toward the TV. "He's too West Coast, or something. I don't know."

"Who?" I asked.

"Igor Bashenko, the guy who was supposed to come to town and become the new director of the Columbus Symphony."

Wass was an icon to the patrons of his saloon, and he often thought this position entitled him to an opinion on everything that affected the community, like a city father or somebody like that. We waited together until the newscaster came back on the tube with the story.

"When his plane landed today," the announcer began, "Igor Bashenko, the newly hired director or the Columbus Symphony was not on it." The voice droned on about the history of the recent orchestra strike and how the previous maestro, Janic Vadea, had stepped down, leaving the leadership slot of the musical institution vacant. A photograph of Vadea appeared on the screen followed by footage of him directing the orchestra last spring at a "Picnic at the Pops" concert, while a recitation of his recent accomplishments at a performing arts festival in Colorado called the Andalucia Festival was touted by the broadcaster. A short clip of an interview with Heinrich Wabstmann, President of the Columbus Symphony, followed.

"Mr. Vadea had great abilities," Wabstmann opined. "Perhaps this new man we hired just has a little trouble keeping time." He chuckled, almost scoffing. "In any event, I'm sure he'll do alright, as soon as we can find him and get him here. He probably missed his plane." He laughed again.

"Do you know the back story on Janic Vadea?" Wass asked me. "Not many people do."

"No, tell me."

"The symphony strike was finally settled by easing him out. He's a suave Serbian with shiny dark hair and impeccably good looks who was known to cavort with all of the richest and most powerful symphony patrons in town. But he also had a reputation as an artistic tyrant who engaged in mental cruelty with his violin players on a regular basis, and it was said, additionally, that he carried on many forms of more playful cruelty with the *Dispatch*'s music critic, Barbara Gamon."

I wondered where Wass got his information. He often came up with behind the scenes stuff like this in lots of different areas, and the fact was, he was usually correct. The Wasserberg family was huge, with maybe 20 different adult grandchildren working in all walks of the city's life. In fact, I knew his aunt, Jenni Wasserberg, who was on the symphony board, but she was 80 years old and really wouldn't be into that sort of gossip.

"So tell me, Wass. You seem to know so much. Why don't you think this maestro would fit in? Tell me the real reason."

"I just don't think he's going to be able to make it with all those aristocrats on the Symphony Board. He comes from a different place than they do. My aunt tells me he composes with technology on the computer, but those blue bloods on the symphony board are practically all from the 19th Century, and into the old masters, not this guy's new age stuff."

"Well, that's going to make my client very unhappy."

"Who?"

"My client, Anastasia Andropov; she's his daughter. Anyway, I've got to go home now. The Arizona game starts at 4:00—"

Just then, Trudy walked back in from her cigarette.

"—and I've got to be on my couch eating my Hershey Bars by then," I said, loudly enough for her to hear.

CHAPTER THREE

I could hardly stand Anastasia's high-pitched voice on the phone, let alone decipher the static her ultra-heavy Russian accent was producing. Her nervous anxiety worsened her English pronunciation as she progressed from simple anxiety to pure anguish, and I had to ask her to repeat almost everything she said more slowly.

Anastasia Andropov and her husband Picup immigrated to Columbus, Ohio, in 1994 from Tashkent, Uzbekistan, one of the former republics of the Soviet Union. They started a chauffeur service in Columbus called "The Picup Andropov Car Service" and I became their lawyer. Picup is just a regular working Joe, a burly bald-headed, vodka-drinking Russian with a stubble beard, who struggles with the English language, but Anastasia is part of the cultural elite of the old Soviet Union, very educated with a degree in nuclear physics from the Moscow State Technicon. As was the case with so many other recent Russian immigrants, she was someone who the professions in American society refused to recognize because her degree was Russian.

Her grandfather, Alexander Bashenko, was an elite Communist Party apparatchik who migrated from Moscow to Tashkent when the entire communist government moved eastward to avoid Hitler's onslaught on Moscow in 1942. There, Anastasia's father, Igor Bashenko, served as maestro of the Tashkent Symphony Orchestra. After coming to this country, he directed the Trans Siberian Orchestra, a very popular juggernaut in the United States. Unfortunately, he is a manic-depressive, and as such has caused his daughter enumerable worries.

I could hardly decipher what Anastasia was saying, she was speaking so fast. Besides that, my attention was diverted. The clamor of the television in the back of my living room wasn't helping much, as the basketball tournament carried on.

"Vinston, Vinston, my papa, he is gone, just gone. I know it. I know it! Maybe in Chicago—where he vas to change planes, maybe not. He vill be on street there, I tell you, even vind up, maybe, in dumpster or something like zat. He can't take care of himself."

Damn! Ohio State just made a 3 pointer, and now, if they could hang on until the buzzer, in 10 seconds they'd beat Arizona to close out my bracket, and go on to the "final four." I'd win $3000, and be in the running for the big enchilada...$6,700 this year at the end of the series. I didn't realize it, but I was leaving the line silent while I was riveted to the TV screen, waiting for that final buzzer.

"Vinston? Vinston!" Anastasia screamed. "Ve came home vith empty limo. He didn't get off plane. You understand me? Do you realize vhat this means? Disaster! It is real disaster."

There it was, the buzzer, and there I was, $3000 richer! I decided I'd put it toward a long overdue vacation with Rosanne. She's my girlfriend, and my accountant, and she really understands me. I need to do something to show her I really care for her after failing to lose the 25 pounds I'd promised to take off, but when you weigh over 300 like me, that's no easy task. Who knows? If OSU becomes the national champ in the final game, with that additional $6,700, we could even maybe go to Europe or something, maybe Italy, which Rosanne has always wanted to see.

"Vinston! Please speak to me!" Anastasia's voice was becoming shrill.

"Yes, yes, so now tell me, Ani, what's all this about your father?"

"C'he's in Chicago," she sniveled. "I checked. C'he vas on plane from San Francisco, and to transfer in Chicago. C'he vas supposed to arrive today for very big greeting. C'he vas on way to Columbus, but in Chicago, c'he just got off plane and kept going into city somewhere instead of making his connection. Now nobody can find him. I know c'he vill perish there if I don't help."

"Why would he do a thing like that, Ani?"

"Chwho knows? *Ya ni znayoo*. I don't know. Crazy, c'he's just crazy. You know vhat I mean, Vinston? You have met him more than once."

My thoughts went back two years ago when Igor Bashenko came to Columbus to visit his daughter and insisted on buying her eight very expensive artistic pieces of glassware from the Chihuly Exhibit at the Columbus Art Museum, for over $400,000, just because he found them intriguing, even though she lives in a tiny house with nowhere to put them, and really could have used that money for more important things. When this man got started with an obsession, he could obsess like nobody else. He got obsessed with the artist, Chihuly. He was also obsessed with computers, ever since learning he could make and mix music with them. When he directed the Trans-Siberian Symphony, even though he'd committed the score to memory, he often had his thin lap-top with him on the music stand so he could watch and measure the frequencies of the sounds the orchestra was making.

"Well, I'm sure he'll be alright," I told Ani. "After all, the man came here all the way from Russia on his own, and he travels all over the country in his profession. I'm sure he can take care of himself."

"Not without his medicines. They came through when his luggage was transferred to flight to Columbus. He just didn't get on plane. Vinston, he takes lithium bicarbonate, and he won't be stable without it for long. Who knows what he'll do? Vhen he came from Russia, they sent him straight from Ellis Island to electro-shock therapy he was so bad off."

"Well, how can I help?" I asked.

"You go to Chicago. You find him. You know many people there, maybe people who could help."

I smoothed my shirt on my ample belly. Her suggestion was impractical. Furthermore, the thought of going back to Chicago created an uncomfortable eruption in my stomach. That city was the venue of the worst events in my life...my divorce, the loss of my little girl, the end of my career as a corporate lawyer...and all because of the improvident disbarment action my former law firm started against me for a mistake they made, not me. I got off, and they paid millions in mal-practice damages. They just went on making more money, but I couldn't get another job because nobody wants to hire a lawyer who's been through disbarment proceedings. I had to leave the city and come back to Columbus. Now I represent corporate clients like The Picup Andropov Car Service and I scrape by doing divorce work and penny ante collections, but my old law firm still represents Exxon. That's what a disbarment proceeding does to your reputation.

"Before I go running off to Chicago, Ani, how about if I make some calls to see if we can't come up with some leads on your father?"

The suggestion seemed to settle her, but my stomach was boiling over at the thought of going back to Chicago. The idea was distasteful.

CHAPTER FOUR

When I walked into my office the following Monday, my phone was already ringing. It was Art Malone, a great hulk of a man with an almost perfectly square face who had made his money with Buckeye Foundries and Steel Co. What white hair he had fringing his bald head was combed straight back and finished in a small pony tail with a silver clasp decorated in the fashion of Navajo art. He was the only member of the elite symphony board who would allow himself to speak to me, probably because of his West Virginia background and his unconventionality in doing just about everything. Once I helped stop a union organizational drive at his business by repossessing the union business agent's car so he couldn't get to the plant to organize the men. Art has felt indebted to me ever since, declaring to all his friends that I am the greatest management "labor lawyer" around. But the rest of the symphony board members consider themselves a cut above him, and definitely too good to be using someone like me as their lawyer.

On the symphony board, Art is anathema, especially to the board president, the straight-laced, German-born Heinrich Wabstmann, President and CEO of Aiden-Life Pharmaceuticals, the largest drug manufacturer in the city of Columbus, and third largest in the United States. The company just went public on the New York Stock Exchange and has been the leader for weeks on the list of 15 stocks followed regularly on the *Columbus Dispatch* business page. According to Art, Wabstmann, a shriveled little man, comes to every symphony board meeting wearing a vest, a silver and black rep tie and a black suit coat, with his glasses toggled on a silver chain. Art wears a cowboy shirt with a string tie, and he has a penchant for turquoise—turquoise cufflinks, a huge turquoise belt buckle, turquoise rings on almost all his fingers, a turquoise string tie holder, and boots with an imbedded turquoise and silver design. The rest of the Board puts up with him simply because he is the symphony's biggest benefactor.

Art hadn't given me any legal work for a long time, but that was about to change. "So what do you think happened out there at the airport this weekend with Igor Bashenko?" he asked.

"I haven't got the faintest," I replied, "but I know it really upset his daughter."

"Well, one person who's plenty happy about it is Janic Vadea. He's a thinkin' he's gonna get his old job back now. Word is, he's not that happy out there in Colorado with that Andalucia Festival or whatever it's called."

"Well, is he going to get his job back?"

"That Rasputin...Over my dead body! The man's too cruel to handle an operation like the Columbus Symphony. Plus, his agreeing to leave is what settled the contract for us. Listen, Winston, Igor Bashenko was scheduled to arrive Saturday at Port Columbus Airport from California to take up the responsibilities of his new position as the Music Director of the Columbus Symphony Orchestra, or what's left of it. The orchestra players just concluded a 23 week strike. The strike was hard fought, so hard, that when Symphony President Heinrich Wabstmann hired scabs to replace the regular musicians, the Ohio Theater was fire-bombed and Janic Vadea was forced to resign as maestro.

"Columbus is now ready for a new Director who can save the city's oldest cultural institution from destruction; Herr Wabstmann is now licking his wounds from his loss of face over the strike; and, the board of trustees, except for Wabstmann, is ready for a new Music Director, but the disaster that occurred last Saturday could change all that. When Bashenko's plane landed without him, everyone was disappointed. The press was there, the symphony concertmaster was there, the Andropov's limousine was there; and, the Columbus Chamber Quartet was present to provide a musical greeting, but Igor didn't get off the plane. Forty or so symphony board of trustees members and their spouses, gathered at the Hyatt on Capital Square to toast the arrival of the new conductor and to break bread with him, but all went home frustrated and disappointed. It was a huge coup to find a replacement who was more well known than Vadea and better than Vadea so quickly. But Bashenko is now a huge political issue on the board, and if something isn't done, instead of Wabstmann being ejected as President, he could regain control."

"Well, what are you going to do about it?" I asked.

"Of course, you know Wabstmann's first move will be to call a meeting of the board for this Friday to rehire Vadea, if he'll come back, which you know he will. Winston, we've got to get Bashenko in here to Columbus, as quickly as possible. You know the family, his daughter and son-in-law, don't you? That could be mighty helpful."

"Yes, his daughter, Anastasia, is already after me to go to Chicago and look for him."

"Well, I think that's a mighty good idea, boy. I want to hire you to do that, and if you find him, I want you to point out to him in a legal sort of a way that he's got a contract to come work here and he needs to fulfill it."

My Toyota Avalon was in no shape for a trip to Chicago. The car, which had been customized to fit my hefty body, had the driver's seat moved back to where the back seat should have been, in order to make room for my bulging thighs, and the driver's seat itself was braced with a steel beam. That modification required all sorts of other changes, such as an extension on the gear selector, a longer steering column and an oversized airbag designed to pin me into the back of the car in case of a wreck. The car was in the shop for repairs on some of these customizations right now. I would have to rent a car or suffer the indignity of buying two seats on an airplane to Midway Airport, and then what would I do? How would I get around in Chicago? Yes, I had Art Malone's promise to pay my bills, but still, I couldn't be too extravagant. So I did the next best thing.

Picup answered the phone when I called. I asked him to get Anastasia because I knew he wouldn't agree to drive to Chicago to look for Ani's father unless she forced him to do so. "Your father, he is like Siberian camel," I'd heard him tell her once before, "indestructible, but always he is spitting, and everywhere he goes he leaves his shit." Picup hated his manic-depressive father-in-law.

"Hello, Ani. I've decided to go to Chicago to look for your father, but either Picup or you will have to drive me in the limo. Tell Picup I will pay the standard day's rental plus all costs for the extra gas and lodging." I figured Art Malone would have no trouble footing the bill and paying my hotel bill.

"Oh, that is vonderful, Vinston. Thank you so much. I vill drive you and Picup will remain at home. That way the amount of time he will have to spend with Papa will be cut down."

"OK, Ani. Let's plan on leaving Wednesday."

"A minute please, Vinston, while I check schedule for the limo. Ve are very busy these days. Wait, I look––Oy yoy! Picup has contracted limo for Wednesday to our biggest client—Mr. Vabstmann, you know, he's big industrialist who manufactures drugs, and he always uses our service for his visitors from overseas. He was already using us all last veekend, except for time ve vent to airport on Saturday to pick up my Papa, who was, as you know a no-show. It embarrassed Picup very much. Ve had donated our car and our time to symphony for zat cause. Anyway, we can go Thursday or Friday instead of Wednesday?"

"OK, Ani, that'll be ok. Let's make it Friday."

"*Xorosho*! Good," she replied.

CHAPTER FIVE

Since we weren't going to leave for Chicago on Wednesday, I decided to take Rosanne out to lunch and tell her about winning the $3000 instead. We met at Buca di Beppo in the Nationwide District.   It's an authentic Italian family style restaurant where they just bring out your order and put it on the table and you serve yourself. I liked it because Rosanne could order a salad, while I ordered wedding soup and the seafood trio which includes shrimp, mussels, marinara and fried calamari, all of which are served family style on a huge platter, which is basically as much as you can eat, and I always eat all of it. Any salad Rosanne doesn't finish, I, of course, also finish. It's also family style. She was peeved when I suggested Buca di Beppo because I had promised to lose weight, and instead I had gained.

"Well, at least you're not insisting we eat at Mozart's Bakery anymore. All those desserts were horrible for you, Winston—linzer torts, chocolate dipped biscotti, napoleons. The only thing good about that place is the piano player.

"Rosanne."

"What did you bring me here for though? To show me how much you can eat?"

"Rosanne."

"You know, you're just kidding yourself, Winston, when you say you'll diet. I think it's time for us to consider another option for you. You lost a lot of weight last year when you were in the hospital, almost 70 pounds, and then you proceeded to gain it all back plus more. Bouncing around like that in the weight department can kill a person. It has simply got to stop. You know gastric bypass surgery isn't a bad option, and you can have it done right here over at the Wexner Medical Center at OSU. I'm beginning to think it's your only option."

"Rosanne." This was beginning to get as bad as it was with Trudy at Wass's bar the other day.

"You just can't seem to control yourself, Winston. You start diets with the greatest of intentions, and you just—"

"RosANNE!!!"

"Yes, Winston, what is it?"

"The reason I brought you here is that it's the most authentic Italian place I know of, and I thought it would be good because I wanted to tell you that we're going to Italy in the fall."

"We're going to Italy? We don't have the money to go to Italy."

"Oh, yes we do."

"How?"

"I won it in March Madness." Well, I hadn't won enough to get us to Italy just yet, but the chances were looking very good that I'd—

"What is March Madness?"

"It's the NCAA college basketball tournament. Almost everybody bets in it, and I'm a winner." *Well, not enough of a winner yet,* I thought, *but I would be.* I had to be now, and if not, I'd get the rest of the money for the trip somewhere else. I was going to show Rosanne that if I couldn't reduce, at least I could produce—earn that is.

"So, Rosanne, will you go to Italy with me? It'll be fun—Rome Venice, Milan, Florence, the running of the bulls!"

"That's in Spain," she corrected, "but, yes, I'll go."

"Good. We'll talk more about it after I get back from Chicago."

You're going to Chicago?"

"Yes, Friday."

"But why?"

"I'll explain when I get back. One of the Columbus Symphony board members, Art Malone, has hired me to do it." I thought I'd keep trying to impress her by dropping Malone's name since I was on a roll.

"Winston, have you talked to Arnold Goldstein about going back to Chicago? Do you really think you're ready for that yet? I'm not sure you can handle it."

I knew why she was concerned. Chicago was where the greatest catastrophe in my life had occurred. Not only had I almost lost my license to practice law there. Not only had I lost my job as a corporate attorney there. But the depression of it all had caused my divorce from my first wife, and when she left, she took my daughter with her. My tactic for avoiding the sadness of it all had been to eat, and to continue to eat until I had gained over a hundred pounds, and then to flee back to my home town of Columbus to eke out a living as a single practitioner doing simple divorces and defending petty criminals and the like. Rosanne had always shown great concern for my mental health. I really couldn't afford to pay for sessions with a psychologist, but Rosanne knew I needed it, so she recommended Arnold Goldstein to me. He was a low cost mental health provider who didn't have an office. Instead, Arnold Goldstein and I talked via Skype every Wednesday at 4:00 p.m. just for quick little psychological tune-ups. It was a lot easier, and cheaper, to get therapy from a talking head on the computer than to pick up and go to an actual office and sit in a waiting room full of disturbed lunatics.

"Well, today's Wednesday, Rosanne, so I guess I will talk to him about it if you think I should."

When I got back to my office, I sat down at the computer, called up Goldstein on Skype, and told him I was going to Chicago and why.

"No, no, and NO, Winston. I don't think you're ready to go back there."

"But why not?" I insisted. "Somebody's got to find Bashenko and convince him to continue on to Columbus, and since he has a contract, it's a legal matter that I can handle as well as any other lawyer."

"Stop thinking about those legal fees, Winston. There are still too many storm clouds there for you, and you'll obsess over everything—maybe even try to look up your ex so you can see your daughter, and when you don't find them, how will you feel? Or if you do find them, how will you feel? As they say, 'Obsession is the stoker of the stalker, and stalking is the stoker of obsession.'"

"Really, I never heard that one before, Arnold."

"Maybe that's because I just made it up."

"Ok, let's discuss something else. How much time do I have left?"

"Five minutes."

"Well, tell me, what would cause a manic-depressive man who is travelling cross country not to board his connecting flight out of Chicago, if his first flight was on time?"

"Could be anything—heart attack, anxiety about his final destination, sudden change of plans, a manic episode of delusion—anything. I don't know, maybe he met a pretty woman on his first flight and just decided to get off the plane with her when it landed. As they say, 'When the penis goes stiff, the mind goes blank.'"

"Is that another saying you just made up, Arnold? If so, I doubt it applies in this case. This man is 65 years old."

Oh, so he's a 65-year-old manic-depressive? That's all the more reason for it to apply—he could be either delusional or hyperactive."

"You think so?"

"Times up, Winston."

CHAPTER SIX

Just then my secretary Marinda came in, or I should say, my "assistant" Marinda. She and I had quite a history. She had worked her way up from a "Mollie Maid," with a contract to clean the office, to being my assistant, whom I leave in charge when I'm out. Besides being absolutely gorgeous, she was efficient and proficient, in everything but typing. For that, I had to purchase a Dragon Natural Speaking Unit in order to get my briefs done.

"Hey, Mr. Attorney who's been out to lunch with his girl when he shouldn't even have been eating lunch. What's up?" she squeaked.

Well, that was just what I didn't need to hear at that moment. It was like every woman I knew was conspiring to shame me into losing weight. Heck, some men go above 350. I was only at 320.

"A lot, what's up with you?"

"A whole lot," she replied, which was something I wasn't expecting to hear.

"Really, what's going on?"

"You first," she teased.

"Well, Rosanne and I are going to Italy."

"What do you mean?"

"It's a long story, and I'll tell you about it later. Tell me, what's been going on here while I was out?"

"That's a long story too, but to cut to the chase, your friend Ronnie Herimus called, and he's all out of joint because of something that happened over at the Arnold Schwarzenegger Fitness Classic...you know...that body building event they have each year at Veteran's Memorial? It seems a dead body they found inside one of the spray booths during the amateur competition was Ronnie's chief competition for the amateur prize. Now they want to award Ron first place, but he doesn't want to take it because he doesn't feel he earned it."

"Yah, I heard about the death. But what do you mean? Ronnie doesn't want to win a pro-am event in body building?"

"Well, yeah, it's very important to him as a personal matter. He says he feels like he's getting 'dirty seconds' in the competition because someone has eliminated the top competitor. Murder is suspected. The police also want to ask him a few questions, something about motive exclusion, and he wants to know what you think. Should he talk to them, or not?"

Ronnie Herimus is my tattooed, muscle-bound friend who's always out of work and doing odd jobs for me. On more than one occasion, those jobs have involved a certain amount of security protection, especially in my earlier days when I was eking out a living by repossessing cars and trucks for the banks. His most prized possessions are his restored '63 Ford Bronco truck, his Harley and his gun collection. But make no mistake. Ron is also a social contributor. Each year, he travels the state on his bike with his biker friends, acting as a sort of honor guard, officiating on Memorial Day, President's Day and Veteran's Day for his favorite organization, Flags of Ohio. He's a weight lifting exercise freak, and this was his third year competing in the Schwarzenegger Classic. On the downside, it seems Ron has always had an instinct for getting himself involved in controversial things involving the police, where he's never at fault but always a suspect. He specializes in guilt by association.

Now it sounded like he was about to become embroiled in another issue with the police.

"Well, is there any sort of prize for this amateur competition he's in?"

"Oh, yeah," Marinda responded, "the prize is $5000 and you become a pro, who can compete in all the pro competitions."

Terrific, I thought to myself. *There's a motive. Never mind that Ronnie would never kill anybody, and the police, who already knew him, also knew that.* "Well, what does he expect me to do about this, Marinda?"

"He says he knows you'll think of something... maybe talk to the police for him or something like that. He said to tell you that maybe if you get Jerry Shapiro and that detective...what's his name Antoine, uh—"

"Anthony Picard?"

"—yah, Picard, assigned to the case, it would help."

"Look, Marinda, lets tell Ronnie I'll do what I can for him. It won't be much. I don't pass out the cases to the gumshoes at the police station. They run their own show. Tell Ronnie that, please! Oh, and tell him I'm not sure Shapiro's the right cop to have on the case, anyway. Also, please get me the substance of the police report concerning the weight-lifter found dead in the spray booth at the Arnold Schwarzenegger Classic."

Within minutes, my efficient Marinda came back with a copy of the police report. The name of the victim was Bruge Biliuss, and he was from somewhere in Belgium. The cause of death was listed as heart attack, but this was before the occurrence of an autopsy. Like many body builders, the man was known for his use of anabolic steroids to increase muscle size but there was something else.

He was suspected of using illegal blood transfusions to raise his red blood cell count in the same way that use of Erythropoietin (EPO) does. The only difference is that blood transfusions can't be detected. Basically, the athlete stores some of his blood when his hemoglobin levels are high, for instance when he is mountain climbing, and then re-infuses the stored blood right before the athletic event. But the increased hemoglobin literally thickens the blood and can lead to cardiovascular problems.

So...end of case, one would think, except for the problem that a syringe with Ronnie's fingerprints all over it was found in the spray booth next to the body. Nobody apparently had bothered to tell Ronnie about this before asking him to comment to the police. Given these facts, there was no way he should talk to them. Ron Herimus was a good friend who had protected me in many situations. It was time to return the favor. He called me "boss" because I had given him so many odd jobs during times when he was down and out without any employment. I had hired him to move me into my apartment on Drexel. I had hired him to take care of my cat; to drive me places that were too far to go on my Moped before I had a decent car, to protect me, sometimes to help me gather evidence, and even to put up one of my friends who was in trouble. When he was in financial trouble, which was at least once every six months, I tried to come up with work for him. I called him.

"I heard you might be in trouble, Ronnie, not just money woes this time, but real trouble. Have you talked to the police yet?"

"No, I was waiting to hear something from Marinda first."

"Good! Well, don't talk to the police. If they want anything from you, tell them you're taking the Fifth until you've got your lawyer with you."

"Oh, Geez, now I'm even more worried."

"Why, Ron? Have you got something to be worried about?"

"No, but—"

I could always tell when Ronnie wasn't being completely truthful. He was just one of those big honest at heart oafs who couldn't tell a lie without getting caught.

"What's this business about a syringe with your fingerprints on it?" I asked

"What? What syringe?"

"The police report says a syringe was found in the spray booth with your fingerprints."

"Well, I'm sure I don't know anything about that," he insisted. "Nobody ever told me about it either."

"Well, just hang tough, Ronnie, my friend. I'm going to Chicago, but I'll be home in a few days." Frankly, I didn't believe him for a minute.

"Boss, I don't know why you're going to be on the road, but I don't want you to shorten your trip on my account."

"Never mind that, Ron. You need a lawyer, and I'm it. What are friends for?"

CHAPTER SEVEN

The Picup Andropov limousine was a black stretch Chrysler, equipped with a bar, a two-way radio, satellite television, the internet, wireless and multiple iPhones. It was rolling northwest toward greater Chicago, at eleven miles to the gallon when we received a call just outside Lafayette, Indiana. A very agitated Picup was yelling in Russian over the phone at Anastasia until she hung up and started crying.

"Chush' sobach'ya!" she muttered, giving the phone the one finger salute.

"Ani, what is it?" I asked.

"It vas Picup. My father called. C'he is staying in a place called Vest Rogers Park, and c'he says he is no longer coming to Columbus. Picup is very glad, but still he is acting like a pig because he hates my father."

"Did Picup tell him we're on the way to Chicago to find him?"

"No, c'he would not do that because he thinks we are stupid to go, and he doesn't want to show my father anybody cares about him."

"Did Igor give the address where he was staying? Did he leave his phone number?"

"No address, but I have phone number. I vill call."

"No wait, Ani. What will you say?"

"I'm telling him we are coming to get him and we vill bring him to Columbus where c'he has a responsibility to fulfill. C'he must not act like a child. The whole world cannot always circulate around him."

"You're going to chastise him?"

"Vell, yes, of course."

"I don't think you should do that, Ani. Remember, he's probably playing a game with us here. Maybe that would be playing right into his hands. He could then aggrandize himself by making you plead for him to come to Columbus. After all, why did he even call in the first place, unless he wanted to toy with somebody over this? No, instead I think we should try talking to him in person wherever he is in Chicago. We'll take him by surprise. But for that, we'll need the address of where he's staying in Chicago. Why not tell him you have his medicines because they came through with his luggage and you need an address to send them to? Here, give me the phone. What's the telephone number? I'll dial while you keep your eyes on the road."

When she got off the phone, Ani was weeping. She had talked to Igor and obtained his address in West Rogers Park, but he had informed her that he was never coming to Columbus, contract or no contract.

"He told me they don't really want him in Columbus, and before he left California, he received calls telling him to stay there if he knows what's good for him."

"Calls from whom, Ani?" I asked.

"He said he knows not. They simply said it's better he stays in California...better for him, better for his career."

"So what are his plans? Where's he going from Chicago? What's he doing in West Rogers Park?"

"He says he knows not yet what he vill do. He vill stay in Rogers Park until he can make decision. He says, place where he stays, this like a safe house for him."

It all sounded pretty dramatic to me..."safe house,"... almost as if somebody had threatened him. I knew manic depressives had a penchant for the dramatic, but really, this all seemed like a cover story for something else. Where was he in West Rogers Park...at a motel...in someone's home? Why West Rogers Park?

"Ani," I asked, "What connections does your father have to West Rogers Park? Does he know anybody there?"

"C'he says he stays with friend...very good friend."

"Do you know of any friends of his from there?"

"No. He never goes there before."

"Did you get the address of this friend?"

"34920 W. Touhy Avenue."

"Good. That's where we'll go."

"C'he says it's a very Jewish neighborhood."

"All the better, maybe my friend, Rabbi Billie Goldman knows somebody there who may be able to help us convince your father to do the right thing and come to Columbus."

My friend Rosanne and I attend Rabbi Billie's Bible Seminars on Sundays. It doesn't matter that I'm not Jewish. I go because of Rosanne and because I just like the discussions we have at Billie's apartment...and the food he serves after them.

"Vinston, religion...it's an opiate. It doesn't help anything. It just makes people feel better. Take it from me. I know. It's like a bad drug."

"That's very Marxist, Anastasia, but I didn't grow up in the former Soviet Union like you."

• • •

Anastasia parked the huge limo, sticking slightly out into the street from the skinny driveway which was too small to accommodate it. The house at 34920 W. Touhy was one story, like all others on the street, built of sandy colored brick with a very shallow hip roof. It had a green front lawn the size of a postage stamp, an undistinguished facade dominated by a large picture window, and a blond wooden door to one side of the window. It was so close to the house next door that the neighbors could have shaken hands by reaching out their side windows. It was also longer than it was wide.

Its unremarkable front door had three small slits toward the top, too high to peek through, which served to let thin shafts of light into the front room. The picture window was heavily draped with a tightly closed green fabric punctuated by hibiscus flowers. The whole effect intimated "nobody's home here." Anastasia rang the doorbell twice, and we waited for a long time without an answer. So I circled around the back to see what I could see.

The windows were sealed, either with drapes or tightly closed venetian blinds. All I could think was that it must be plenty dark in there. Only one small sign of life, a sound like experimental notes from a moog synthesizer, was issuing from the back windows. It could have been Igor composing on his computer. I returned to the front stoop to find Anastasia completing a note, intended for the mail slot in the door, telling her father that we were in town and would be staying at the Seneca Hotel in Evanston where he could reach us.

As she pushed the message through the mail slot, the door suddenly opened just wide enough to permit its chain lock to reach full extension. A tired, exotic-looking female face in its late fifties peeked through the opening.

"Yes?" The voice was low. "Who is it?"

"Read the note," Anastasia answered.

A long silence ensued, presumably while the note was being digested by the woman on the other side of the door. "Just a minute," she grumbled. Then another long silence ensued, presumably as she went to show the note to Igor. Finally, the door was unlocked and we were allowed in with great reluctance on the woman's part.

The interior of the modest home was the exact opposite of its exterior—Miro prints hanging everywhere, with heavy wooden Russian Orthodox religious icons sitting around on the tables. In a niche between the living room and the dining room, hung a small pencil Picasso cartoon, delicately framed. An ornate table, covered with a gold-braided cloth, in front of the draped picture window, served as a pedestal for a large brass samovar bearing the seal of Czar Nicholas II embossed on top of one of the handles, and there was a bone china tea set surrounding it. In the corner on a raised podium stood a Steinway baby grand piano with a gold leaf harp next to it, and two ornate music stands.

"I'll be out in a minute," announced a sing-song male voice apprehensively, from what must have been a bedroom to the side of the living room-dining room complex. "Just let me turn this computer off." Then, Igor Andropov, dressed in a red silk bathrobe with a paisley design and brown leather slippers, the kind without any uppers on the heels, appeared in the hallway and walked out into the living room like he owned the place. He looked at Anastasia, eyes twinkling, and embraced her. "I knew you would come," he said to her, "as soon as you asked me for an address to which to send my medicine, but I didn't think you'd get here so soon."

"You vanted me to come, didn't you?" Ani replied.

Igor ignored the question. "This is my friend Ida," he said, turning toward the woman who'd let us in. "And this is Ida's house, or, I should say, Ida's husband's house. He's away in Europe right now."

For the first time, I noticed that the woman was wearing a black negligee, covered by a filmy chiffon robe, untied at the waist. Obviously, they'd been lounging together. Probably in her late 50's or early 60's, she was a thin, well-developed woman, preserved by surgery in all the right places. She smiled and nodded, trying to look demure without any real success. Ida was obviously too worldly for that. "Would you like some tea?" she asked. "I have Black Russian Chai." There was a tiny hint of an accent in her voice.

"I didn't know you had friends in Chicago," Ani persisted.

"I didn't. I met Ida on the plane from San Francisco."

"And you just decided to get off the plane vith her c'here in Chicago and stay at her house?" Ani chided.

Igor ignored this question also. "Ida is very musical, as you can see," he said, pointing to the baby grand and harp, "and I'm really glad you're meeting her. We have much in common. She is Russian too. The reason I knew you would come is when you asked for my address there was no need to mail my medicine to me. As you know, I could have had the doctor call a replacement prescription into any drug store. You wanted the address so you could find me, my dear, and, of course, as you can see, I let you find me."

"*Otetz,* vhy do you do things like this?" The frustration welled in Anastasia's voice, and the two of them burst into Russian, back and forth at each other with Igor shaking his head "no," and Ani bobbing her head up and down, "yes."

"Nyet, Nyet!"

"Da, Da, DA!"

Finally, I spoke up interrupting them. "Mr. Bashenko, I have been asked by a very important man in Columbus, Art Malone, to come out here and bring you back to be the director of the Columbus Symphony Orchestra."

"Ah yes, Mr. Malone. He's a good man, very well meaning. And Mr. Wabstmann, did he send you too?"

I didn't answer.

"I thought not," Bashenko continued. "You see, there is...how do you call it?...a rift on the symphony board. Half of them want me to come there, and half of them don't. It's very difficult, very complicated. And you might say that someone from Columbus has contacted me and disinvited me to come there."

"Oh, there are always factions," I responded. "Any time you get more than three people together and give them any sort of power, politics abides. But they gave you a written contract didn't they? That means the majority wants you there."

"It's your responsibility, *Otetz*," Ani added. "You have a responsibility to come to Columbus now and to be Music Director. I know you vill do good job."

"He's been threatened not to come," Ida piped up.

"Threatened? What do you mean, threatened?" I asked.

"You know, his life...threatened," Ida asserted. "He's in great danger."

"And c'how would you know this?" Ani insisted.

"Because he told me," Ida replied. "We are in love."

"Ach!" Ani turned around throwing up her hands. She headed for the door, and I followed her. When we got outside, she stalked over to the limo and sat in the driver's side. "Vell, that does it," she spat. "C'he's at it again and there's little ve can do."

"At what again, Ani?" I asked. "What do you mean? What's he doing?"

"Vhat's c'he doing? I'll tell you vhat he does. C'he tells vild stories to make himself seem in need, and to make himself seem exciting, so he can pick up women. C'he told her c'he vas threatened and she fell for it and vants to take care of chim...like an exciting naughty little boy who's in trouble. C'he lied to her to stimulate her sympathies. C'he used to do it with my mother after c'he cheated on her. C'he's been doing it also in one form or another ever since my mother died. C'he vill do anything to, how you say, make a woman's pants fall down. Two years ago, c'he vas bringing young Russian vomen to America to marry them, so they could become citizens. Then, vhen he was finished, they divorced. Don't you see, Vinston, c'he is very sick man. Now he has caught himself up vith this whore, Ida."

"You mean, the only reason he's not in Columbus where he should be is because he's on a lark with Ida?"

"Da."

"Well we've got to do something about that. We can't just let it be." *When the penis goes stiff, the mind goes blank. How could that talking head of a psychologist, Arnold Goldstein, have correctly predicted this?* I thought to myself.

"But vhat can we do, Vinston? C'he's crazy. It's his disease."

"I don't know. Tell me more about him. What's he like? What are his passions? To what kind of people is he likely to listen? Does he know the difference between right and wrong?"

"His passion is music, of course," Ani began, "and he's religious, very religious, almost to point of superstition, vith strong sense of right and wrong, very spiritual, but he just goes crazy from time to time, and then he always seeks to be forgiven for it."

Suddenly, I had an idea. Tomorrow, I would call my rabbi, Billie Goldman.

He always had a semi-applicable parable from the Old Testament, and sometimes it even helped.

CHAPTER EIGHT

Billie Goldman was an ordained rabbi who had spent six months in jail for fencing stolen goods. It's a long story which there's no time to tell now. Suffice it to say I represented him when it happened, and he is now my rabbi. I'm not Jewish, but everyone should have a rabbi. Billy's the one who made the *Shidduch*, as he would call it, or match, between Rosanne and me. I sometimes turn to him for advice when I have no ideas of my own, and he comes up with a story from the Old Testament that, believe it or not, seems to apply.

"You say this Mr. Bashenko loves music above all else, yet he prefers to fornicate in Chicago, rather than bring the musical beauty he can make to the Columbus Symphony, and he blames the symphony board for his decision. And, this man is Jewish? Hm... reminds me a little of the story of David and Bathsheba. Do you know it?"

"Tell me."

"King David took another man's wife, Bathsheba, while the man was away, and later had the man sent to his death. He then married Bathsheba. But the Prophet Nathan reproved him with a story about the richest man in the kingdom, who could have had anything he wanted, yet he took away the one little lamb of his neighbor for himself, to the exclusion of all others. 'What would you do to this man, Nathan?' asked the king. 'Kill him,' David replied, self- righteously. Then Nathan applied the case directly to King David's act with Bathsheba."

"What happened?"

"What happened? The guilt Nathan brought down on King David resulted in the famous 51st Psalm of confession and renewal. David sang in contrition: 'Have mercy on me, God, in accordance with your merciful love; in your abundant compassion blot out my transgressions... For I know my transgressions; my sin is always before me... A clean heart create for me, God; renew me with a steadfast spirit, and I will teach the wicked your ways, that sinners may return to you...'"

"I don't get it, Billy. What is it you're trying to say?"

"What am I trying to say? Confront him with the moral wrong he's doing. Blame him. Make him feel guilty. Tell him he can redeem himself by going to Columbus and returning to his music. Mention the 51st Psalm to him. If he's a truly religious Jewish man, he'll recognize it as one of the central prayers of the Day of Atonement. He'll give up this woman and continue on to Columbus. He'll substitute his music for God's place in the parable."

"Did King David give up Bathsheba?"

There was silence at the other end of the line. "Just try it," Billy said, "it might work, even if he brings her along with him to Columbus."

But how could we deliver such a message to Igor? I wondered. *How could we get the story of David and Bathsheba across to him in a manner transmitting its correct meaning and causing him to take the right action?* This man did not have all of his oars in the water. Who knew what voices he listened to. Then it came to me. I thanked Billy and made another call after hanging up.

"You what?" Trudy responded incredulously. "You want me to break into this poor slob's computer and make him think he's receiving a message from God by email?" She slammed the phone down on me, but I called her back.

"Trudy Fischel, you can do this! You're the queen of all computer hackers, and he's not a poor slob. He's going to be the new director of the Columbus Symphony Orchestra. He's already a famous orchestra conductor."

"Well, God help the Columbus Symphony! And what am I supposed to be... the angel Gabriel, or should I say Gabriella? Winston, honey, believe me, I can see how you might fantasize about me, especially in bed at night, after you've dropped Rosanne off, with my fluttery white wings, skimpy sarong barely covering my sexy tattoos, and my not so bad legs, but I'm neither an angel nor a magician. How do you expect me to keep him from tracing a stupid email like that back to me?"

I could just imagine her lighting up a cigarette and ashing all over the bar at Wass's as I was talking to her. She was only acting put off by the idea. I knew in reality that the challenge appealed to her. "Oh, I wouldn't worry too much about that, Trudy. Igor Bashenko is more a romantic than a doubter. Believe me, he's far more spiritual than practical, a perfect candidate for the supernatural rather than the technical. He won't even try to trace the email. Let's face it, he's crazy. Besides, Trudy, this is your opportunity to make a great contribution to the cultural growth of our city. The man's a musical genius."

"Let's hope music is his only genius. Otherwise, I could wind up in jail. How would I even do this? What could I even say? The idea of a computer bringing somebody a message from Heaven is intriguing though."

"I don't know," I answered. "You'll think of a way. Maybe you could make it sound biblical. Burst on to his screen with something that says, "AND AS YOU BEHOLD THE COUNTENANCE OF IDA IN ALL HER BEAUTY, LIKE THE ANCIENT LION OF JUDAH SEEKING SATISFACTION, REMEMBER THE STORY OF DAVID AND BATHSHEBA AND SEEK REPENTANCE! Then tell the story, and tell him what he needs to do."

"Hmm, lemme get back to you on this," Trudy said. "I'll need to think about it...what font to use, what colors, whether to inject a few Hebrew letter characters, etc."

Great! Trudy's response was positive. She would do it. Just as I was hanging up on my call to her, my cell rang. It was Marinda.

"They arrested Ronnie Herimus last night as he was pulling up to the window at the White Castle on Kenney and Henderson," she reported. "They didn't even give him time to pick up the sliders he'd ordered."

"What was he doing at the White Castle?"

"Nothing, he says, just picking up four hamburgers, fries and a shake."

If they'd arrested Ronnie at a White Castle, that meant they must have been following him for a while before the arrest. There's nothing special about White Castle. It's just a Columbus icon where you can get the best bite-sized hamburgers in the world, the first hamburger chain in the United States. But why had they been following him? What more was there to the story of the syringe with Ron's fingerprints that had been found in the tanning booth?

"Marinda," I said, "Look, I can't leave Chicago right now. Tell Ronnie I know how uncomfortable it's going to be for him in jail for a few days. But I won't be able to get there in time for his bond hearing."

I had to wait for Trudy to play God with Igor on the computer, so I could bring him back if he was going to come. Meanwhile, my friend Ronnie would be languishing in jail. I felt horrible about that.

"Not a problem, boss. I'll go to the bond hearing for him in your place."

"But, Marinda, you haven't got a license to practice law, you'll—"

"That's ok, I've got other stuff. Do you think Rosanne can scrape together the money to pay a bail bondsman once bail is set?"

"That depends on what it's set at, but you—"

"I'll do just fine, boss. Remember, I couldn't type when I became your secretary. I was just a Mollie Maid. Now, I'm a paralegal. I think I can get him released on his own recognizance if we get the right judge."

"I doubt that, Marinda. What are you going to say?"

"It's not what I'm going to say, boss. It's what I'm going to wear. I'm just going to be me. I've noticed that works down at the courthouse very well for me. Of course, I assume I may drop your name, right?"

"Sure. Be my guest."

CHAPTER NINE

"You heard me," Art Malone said. "An epiphany; he says he's had an epiphany!"

"An epiphany," I marveled. "What do you mean?"

"I don't know. He just called me last night and said he was sorry he didn't show up last Saturday at the airport when he was supposed to. But since then, God had spoken to him, or some such thing, and now he's decided to come to Columbus and perform his functions under the Music Director's contract."

I continued acting surprised, knowing all the time that Trudy had succeeded in performing her magic by hacking into Igor's computer with the so called "message from God" we had prepared for him. The plan was working. Rabbi Billy's interpretation of the 51st Psalm was working. "That's pretty hard to believe," I told Art. "Did he say anything else?"

"Only that it was the only way he could blot out his transgressions and repent, or some sort of drivel like that."

Yep, I thought to myself, *Trudy's dirty work had succeeded*. Igor was seeing a return to the professional musical world in Columbus as his repentance for doing Ida while her husband was away. "So is there anything you want me to do?" I asked Art.

"While I don't suppose so," Art replied. "I guess, just make sure he gets to Columbus as quickly as possible. Nobody expected this turn of events, and you've done a good job, getting out there to Chicago and finding him and all. I'm still going to cover all your expenses, but for now, I've got to get off this phone and tell that little Heiny, Wabstmann, to call off the emergency meeting he's set up with the symphony board. They're planning to rehire Janic Vadea as maestro, you know, because they think Bashenko has breached his contract."

I hung up from Malone very satisfied with myself. *An epiphany, huh; I had created an epiphany and it was going to save the Columbus Symphony Orchestra.* I couldn't help but be pleased. Now the only thing left to do was to go over to Ida's house, collect Igor, and get on the road with him back to Columbus in the limo.

But that turned out to be more involved than I had guessed at first blush. Ida's married name was Dzugashvili, shortened to Dzugash after her husband Joseph's arrival in the United States. Half Cossack, he was born in a small town in what is today the Republic of Georgia, near the Chechen border. Ida was born in Moldova to a Jewish family named Routman, and she came to the United States when she was only two. They met in Chicago when Ida was 18 and Joseph Dzugash was 29, and they married shortly thereafter. Joseph got reasonably rich as the representative of an arms manufacturer, traveling the world for his employer. He assuaged his wife's resentment about his age and constant absences by spoiling her. She was used to having anything she wanted, and in this case, she wanted Igor Bashenko.

She was also a fighter. In the tradition of most Georgian males, when Joseph was home, he beat her and required her to wait on him hand and foot. Their relationship over the years had been a powder keg, and she could get very emotional. She also knew how to be stubborn and protective of herself.

Now Ida was madder than a queen hornet whose hive had been wrecked. "He can't leave," she screamed. "I won't let him. I won't allow it!"

"Vell, he's going to leave, like it or not," Anastasia retorted, "and there's nothing you can do about it. Igor Bashenko is my *otetz*, and he is coming back to Columbus with us."

"We'll see about that," Ida spat, as she grabbed Igor, dragging him away with her. "He may be your father, so you can call him *otetz*, but he's my *lyubit*, you understand, my lover," she announced defiantly. Strange sounds of hollering began issuing from behind the closed door of the bedroom into which she pulled Igor. They were in there for forty-five minutes, until Igor came out sheepishly, but looking very happy.

"I'm not going," he announced, as Ida threw him a self-satisfied grin.

"Oh, yes you are," Anastasia said. "It's what's supposed to be. You know that."

Igor glanced toward his computer in the bedroom, obviously ambivalent. Then he glanced at Ida who began rubbing his chest with her ringed fingers and with her face close to his, talking so nobody else could hear.

"Bring Ida with you," I said. "Why don't you bring her with you?"

"I can't do that," Ida protested. "I can't just leave here. I have a home. My husband will be home in a month."

"So what?" said Igor. "You don't want to be with him anyway. It's me you want to be with, so why not? We can play Dvorjak together in Columbus and Rachmananov. We'll have the piano and the harp shipped to us. We can do everything together, and I will make a wonderful life for you in Columbus. Leave your husband and come with me."

Ida looked at Ani, and then at me with pain in her face as if she was actually considering dumping Joseph Dzugash after almost 40 years of marriage and becoming a new woman. "What's in Columbus?" she demanded. "What will there be of attraction to me there besides Igor?"

The first things that came to mind were the OSU Buckeyes with their football and basketball teams, but that would never do for an answer to this woman I quickly decided. "Why don't you come and see?" I said. "If you don't like it, you can always leave. I used to live in Chicago like you, and I left the life I had here for Columbus. I've never regretted it, and I don't think you will either."

"Will you take care of me if I come with you Igor Igorovich?" she asked.

"Oh yes, my dear."

And that was it. Within two hours, she'd packed her suitcases, and the four of us were on the road in the black limousine, headed toward Buckeye town. Ani and I rode together in the front seat for a while, talking. "What do you suppose caused Ida to decide so quickly to leave Chicago for Columbus with your father?" I asked.

"Who knows? Both of them, they are crazy," she quipped. "She is probably manic-depressive too, like him. Sex is big driver for people with that disease."

Again my mind wandered back to Arnold Goldstein's diagnosis...*When the penis goes stiff, the mind goes*—The iPhone in the limo rang suddenly interrupting my thought.

"Win, it's me." It was Ronnie Herimus. "I'm out. They let Marinda appear for me. We pled not guilty."

"Well, I'll be a...What did they charge you with?"

"Manslaughter."

"What did she get them to set your bail at?"

"$600,000. We got a surety bond from a bail bondsman at 15%"

"Whoa! That's a low bail for that type of offense, but still too rich for somebody like Rosanne to scare up the money for...$65,000. I presume you guys went to Rosanne for the money. That's what I told Marinda to do, I think. I can't really remember."

"We didn't have to go to Rosanne. Before Marinda could even meet with her, some outfit I don't know the name of paid the bond for me."

"Who are they?"

"No idea, boss. Marinda's checking into it now. By the way, she did a great job at the hearing. She wore her tight-fitting, short, black dress with a scoop neck, heels and no stockings. The judge couldn't stop looking at her."

"No wonder you got away with such a low bail, but still...manslaughter, that's not good, Ron. When I get back, I'm going to take you to the best criminal lawyer in town."

"No, boss. I want you to defend me. You'll do just fine."

I looked over at Anastasia who was contentedly driving us to the southeast, purring Russian songs under her breath. I would collect no fee for it from her, but I had gotten her the result she wanted. Her father would be in Columbus directing the symphony. Behind the driver's wall in the back of the limo, Ida and Igor were busy groping each other like teenagers. They were getting what they wanted too, as was Art Malone.

CHAPTER TEN

Ronnie Herimus was my biggest *pro bono* client, and now he was asking me to take on what could turn out to be a murder case before all was said and done. I had never represented anyone in a homicide before.

A criminal lawyer never asks his client if he did it. He doesn't want to know, because if he knows his client's guilty, he's got a mess on his hands, one that can lead to disbarment, either for failing to vigorously defend the client or for suborning perjury, especially if he puts his client on the stand and knowingly lets him lie. The lawyer is in a bind between his ethical obligations as an officer of the court to follow the rules and seek justice, and his duty to his client under the attorney-client privilege to protect confidential communications. Resigning prior to trial is not the answer and, indeed, the court may not permit him to resign. At the very least, a lawyer who knows his client did it, must conduct a trial religiously holding the prosecution to the "beyond a reasonable doubt" standard for conviction. At worst, he might conduct an aggressive defense, damaging the reputations of prosecution witnesses he knows to be telling the truth with brutal cross examination and leaving false suggestions, without any evidence, that others than his client committed the crime. These rules can also lead to a dangerous dance between lawyer and client where the client demands that he testify and the lawyer can't talk him out of it. They can also lead to fierce chastisement of the lawyer by the public and his own legal community.

Ronnie slouched in the chair on the other side of my desk. This was the first time I'd been in the office in over a week, the first time I'd actually been able devote my undivided attention to his case. I kept asking him about the drug he was accused of giving Bruge Biliuss in the spray booth, thinking it was some sort of performance enhancer. What was it called? I wanted to know, not did he administer it to Biliuss, but what was the name of the drug they found in Biliuss' system? What were its properties? Where could it be obtained? But Ronnie just kept insisting he was never in the spray booth and had no idea about any drug. I figured since the charge was manslaughter, not murder, it wouldn't be so bad if I learned Ronnie had administered the drug, not so bad that is, so long as he didn't realize this particular type of performance enhancer could kill. The issue was, after all, did he give Biliuss the drug *intending* to kill him, or just intending to help him perform better. But Ronnie, knowing that taking illegal drugs at the show was a disqualifying offense that could get him barred from future competitions, seemed bound and determined to *know nothing* about any drug or any syringe.

"The syringe had your fingerprints on it, Ron," I kept saying. "We need an explanation."

"I don't know anything about that," he kept responding. "I never touched that syringe, and I don't know how it got into that spray booth, boss. I was never in there."

Believe me, as a lawyer who'd experienced a disbarment proceeding once already, I was plenty happy he was taking this tack, even though it was going to make it harder to defend him if I couldn't find out these facts. Now all I had to do was believe him, and I was in the clear as far as any ethical question might go. I couldn't be disbarred under the cannons of ethics for knowingly suborning perjury.

"OK, Ronnie," I said, "let's take a different tack. On the day Bruge Biliuss was found dead, tell me everything you did from the time you got up in the morning in sequence—where you went, what you did, and who may have seen you do it."

"You sound like you don't believe me, boss. What's going on here?"

"No, I'm just looking for possible clues as to how someone else might have gotten your fingerprints on that syringe." The answer was not enough for him. He was insulted.

"OK," he said. "I got up. I fed my cat. Actually, it's your damn cat. He's been living with me ever since Rosanne announced she was allergic to cats."

"I'm sorry about that, Ron. I'll come over and pick Sachmo up tomorrow."

"Now there you go again, jumping to conclusions, Win. Actually, Sachmo's no problem and I love him, even if he is a diabetic pain in the ass. Anyway, after feeding him, I ate breakfast, and...actually, come to think of it, I had a visitor that morning for a little while, some guy from a pharmaceutical company trying to get me to try their steroids. Steroids aren't illegal substances, you know. He said he was going around visiting all the guys high up in the amateur standings down at the Schwarzenegger Show, trying to get us to use their stuff, figuring the winner would turn pro, and if he was on their drug at the time, his company could get a nice cheap endorsement out of it. He told me my chief competition, Bruge Biliuss, had refused to use the drug, so the road was open and clear to me to get a nice fat endorsement contract if I used the drug and won the competition."

"What was his name?"

"I can't remember. I can't remember his company either, Pharmacy something or other, I don't know. Anyway, after he left, I went out to the garage to finish changing the rods in my Bronco. She's gonna be really sweet when I get that engine of hers rebuilt."

Ronnie's Ford Bronco was his most prized possession. He was always working on it and he kept it really pristine, but he hardly ever took it out of the garage. He never drove it, except in Fourth of July parades.

"Wait a minute, wait a... Did you say some company paid your bond?"

"Yah, boss, some outfit did, I don't know who. Anyway, after I finished with the rods, I went down to the Schwarzenegger Show at Vets Memorial and hung out."

Something was really strange here. Ronnie seemed to want to gloss over that point awfully fast. I decided to just let him for now, to see what else I could pick up as he carried on with his stream of consciousness.

"With whom, Ron?" Who did you hang out with at the Schwarzenegger Show that afternoon?"

"With who? Oh, geez, I don't know, just a bunch of the girls—all women body builders."

"So, you were on the women's side of the floor, not the men's"

"Definitely."

Ronnie was shamelessly incorrigible when it came to looking for ladies, his favorite haunts being the Giant Eagle Supermarket, the public library and the ABC Bowling Alley. The Schwarzenegger Show provided him with a whole new killing field once a year, and it was especially attractive to him since so many of the girls were so well worked out.

"Who'd you spend most of your time with down there that afternoon?"

"Awe, a girl I'd met long before, I'm afraid. She was the best of the lot. I'd met her last year in a Christian Science Reading Room. You know? That's a great place to meet single women."

"Did you ever go over to the men's side?"

"Only once, and that was to check what time my show was starting the next day."

"Who did you talk to on the men's side?"

"Just the administrative guy at the table there. I don't know his name."

I called Marinda in and asked her if she would please check to see who all the vendors were at the Schwarzenegger Show, especially drug vendors. I also asked her to do a computer search for steroids used by athletes, especially body builders. I wanted to know who manufactured them.

Then, I had Ronnie drive me down to Vets Memorial to show me the tanning booth where it all happened.

"Actually, they're more than tanning booths, boss. They're spray booths. You can go into them and tinge yourself with green highlights if you want, or sparkles, or even just olive oil to make yourself appear all sweaty."

"Why would you want to do that?"

"Image, boss, it's all image. Maybe you're wearing green trunks, so you want to tinge yourself green in the backlight that's shining on you while you flex to make yourself look better. There are certain points the judges all look at in your musculature, but in the end, it's always who looks the best overall. Who is the most interesting, and sometimes the judges are female."

"So, do you do that too, Ronnie?"

"No, I don't use the spray booth because I have tattoos, and I figure that should be enough fluff for the judges. I just wipe myself down with various oils that highlight them. I believe it's the flex, not the sex that counts anyways."

While we were talking, Marinda came in with a message to call Igor Bashenko. When I returned his call, he told me that already he'd run into some very grave difficulties in his new symphony director's job. Could I help him?

CHAPTER ELEVEN

"The symphony board rehired me, and that's all I know about it. So, that's why I am standing here on this podium holding this baton right now. You'll have to talk to Heinrich Wabstmann about it," the smug Serbian advised.

Janic Vadea stood in the practice room, perched on the conductor's podium in the midst of the Columbus Symphony Orchestra, like a hawk surveying possible candidates for lunch. His dark eyes leered from beneath his shining black pompadour like security cameras focusing on a criminal. Now he would take his retribution for the strike. Now that he'd been rehired, a dark purge in the violin section was about to occur, and he would dismiss the brass player in the back whose playing had never been to his liking. It would all happen over time, so as not to raise any suspicions.

"But I do not hesitate to remind you, Mr. Vadea," Igor protested, "that I am the one with a written contract to lead this group, sir, and I have brought my lawyer with me to so inform you."

At Igor's request, I had accompanied him to the rehearsal to help him claim his job. The orchestra players were all watching in amazement as the battle ensued.

"Ah, Mr. Bashenko, but you did not show up for your debut, instead choosing to breach your contract, and when you did that, the symphony board went ahead and rehired me, which was a wise decision I might add."

"But I was told the meeting where you were to be rehired was cancelled," I protested.

"Oh, and by whom? Who told you a thing like that?"

"Art Malone."

"Ah, Art," Vadea laughed, "the Navajo Indian of the Columbus Symphony Board, with all his turquoise baubles. He must have been using his dream catcher when he told you that. It never happened. Heinrich Wabstmann went through with the meeting over Mr. Malone's protests, and, sorry, but yours truly was reappointed Music Director."

"But, Wabstmann knew at the time that Mr. Andropov here was on his way to Columbus to take up his post, even though he had not arrived when first scheduled."

A rumble of discussion rippled through the players as they sat there gaping at the confrontation taking place in front of them.

"I don't know anything about that. You would have to contact Mr. Wabstmann on that subject." And with that, Vadea turned to the waiting players, tapped his baton on his music stand like a high school band leader, and said, "OK, let's take it from the full rest after the first bar. Remember, allegro, allegro! I want it allegro." And he raised his arms to strike the first beat. It was to be Mozart's *15th in G Major*.

But there was silence as his baton came down. "We want Mr. Bashenko," said concert master Miriam Jaspers, as she loosened her bow and placed it on the trough at the bottom of her music stand, refusing to play. The entire violin section followed suit. Then, the tuba player in the back let out a huge blat from his instrument and released a gob of hawker from his spit valve onto the floor. The trombone section blew a long downward sliding note, and the timpani player beat out the old theme from the TV show Dragnet on his drums.

"Time to step down, Mr. Vadea," I counseled. "Sounds like it's time to step down."

Vadea's eyes narrowed; his jaw clenched; and he broke his baton in half, throwing it at his feet. A look of utter hatred appeared on his face and he mumbled an explicative, adding, "We'll see about this." Then he turned and walked out. The orchestra players began to applaud. The concert master picked up her bow, tightening it, and Igor Bashenko mounted the podium to lead the orchestra for the first time.

"Ok, my children," he said, "lightly now like we're all happy." And, he raised his arms and gave the down stroke.

Rosanne, who'd come along to watch the fireworks, after hearing my explanation for rushing off to Chicago, was standing at the door as Vadea exited with the orchestra playing in the background. "I'd like to be a bug on the wall at the next symphony board meeting," she told him. Vadea jutted his chin out without really looking at her, and pretended to have trouble getting around her in the doorway. As the orchestra ended the first movement, I heard Igor instructing his new troupe.

"Ok, now we'll try something a little out of the ordinary. Everyone close your music. We're going to play it again from memory. Oh, I know many of you haven't memorized your scores, but don't worry. You've practiced this many times before, so play it from your hearts. Play what you feel. Don't be afraid to miss this or that cue. I will cue you. Watch me. And, if you forget a repeat, or you miss some notes, or play too loudly, no problem. Watch me and the signs I give you. I want to hear what this thing sounds like when you're playing what you feel, not what the music says you should play."

I watched Igor as he began the experiment, his bald head shining in the lights with the unruly fringes of white curly hair on either side. His swaying arms were lilting the melody along, while his lips were playing out the counterpoint to the woodwind section...pa, pa, pa, PA, pa pa...p'pa, p'pa, p'pa, p'paaa...then he would cue the brass...Baroom, barroom, baroommm...and then the timpani...boom...the man was having fun, and the players were really into it! It was a far cry from what his predecessor had produced.

Turning to Rosanne, I whispered, "The meeting of the board will be a bloodbath. This man's too unconventional for them. They're going to do everything they can to get rid of him, maybe even to the point of getting a restraining order, restraining him from conducting."

"What can you do about it?" Rosanne asked.

"I don't know. Maybe I can get Art Malone to take me to the meeting with him. We'll insist on Igor's contract rights. I'll explain to them that they may be able to get a court order banning him from directing the orchestra, but no court can force the players to play if they have a director for whom they refuse to play."

"But what about the labor laws?" Rosanne asked. "Isn't that a strike...an illegal strike?"

"I don't know. They say the only thing that settled the last strike was the board's promise to get rid of Vadea."

"But that's not in writing, is it?" Rosanne pointed out.

"Still, if the players won't play for him, how can any court make them do so? And if it tries to, how can a court make the players play well? I think we've got the upper hand here."

"But the Board could just fire them all and hire replacements," Rosanne insisted.

"I don't think so. They're highly skilled labor. Where is the board going to find so many replacements? It's more likely Columbus would go without another symphony season. The board members would be cutting off their noses to spite their faces. They're over a barrel."

"But those board members are all big business owners and rich people. There are some pretty big egos there, and it's unlikely they'll let the players, or Bashenko, get away with this if they really don't want him. You know what they say, 'If you want a fight, back a tiger into a corner.'"

Rosanne was right. It was a real conundrum.

CHAPTER TWELVE: BACK TO THE PRESENT

The morning after the shooting, I arrived at the Bashenko condo to find Ida absent along with all of her clothes and jewelry. Anastasia had gone to the Wexner Medical Center where her father was on a ventilator. He was still alive, but the internal bleeding was bad and had thrown him into shock. Picup was at the Police Station supposedly filling them in on what little he knew about the background of Igor Bashenko. Actually, he was just spreading lies about the man, whom he had hated ever since marrying Anastasia. He had just about succeeded in convincing them that Igor was still a communist who could not be trusted when a lieutenant entered the room with a dossier on the musician indicating he'd left Tashkent on the run to avoid being taken to one of Stalin's gulags. Years ago, someone had denounced him as a traitor to the Stalinist cause because of his penchant for the works of the anti-communist composer Dimitri Shostakovich. The police wound up taking down everything Picup said and then disregarding it—blowing him off, so to speak.

Back at the Bashenko condo, the *Columbus Dispatch* lay at the threshold to the door, headline up, with size 32 font proclaiming, "Maestro Shot at Debut." In smaller sub-heads, the newspaper announced: "4 Shots Fired, Only One Finds Its Mark—Terrorism Not Ruled Out."

My cell suddenly sounded with the first few bars of the Ohio State fight song, indicating I had a text message. "Well, what do you think?" The message from Art Malone played out on my screen.

"I don't know, Art," I texted back. "What do you think?"

"What do I think?" he replied. "I think Heinrich Wabstmann tried to contact Janic Vadea this morning to take over the rest of the season for Bashenko. I also think he got no answer, because Vadea has suddenly departed Columbus. At least, that's what my people tell me. I sent them over to his hotel to look for him."

"Well, where do you think he went, Art?"

"I'd like to think he's left to continue his new role out in Colorado at the Andalucia Festival, but something tells me that's not the case, because the hotel says it put through two overseas calls to Belgrade last night and one long distance call this morning to the Serbian Consulate in Cleveland. He's a Serbian citizen, and I think he's going back there."

"So what are you saying, Art?"

The words came out slowly and the answering text was long. "I'm saying the police need to know all of this, as well as the background between Vadea and Bashenko, including their little face-off awhile ago in the practice room in front of the orchestra, and I further think that I'm not the right person to give it to them."

My thumbs began racing over the keyboard of my phone. "Art, please, I don't want to get involved."

"But you are involved, Barchrist," came the reply. "You've got to man up. You're the only one who can give the cops the background on the intrigue going on at the board of trustees behind closed doors on this thing. That disgraceful little Heine Herr Wabstmann is one of the chief actors here, I'm sure of it, but nobody can really say that except you. That damn Hun runs half this town and he's always got his fangs out. He's above nothing when it comes to securing his own power."

"Well, you could tell the police all this too, Art," I protested.

"Oh, no, no, no, my lawyer friend. That would be highly inappropriate. Besides, that's why I hired you."

I left the Bashenko condo and went to the hospital. When I arrived, Anastasia Andropov was waiting for me.

"She's a devil, a *mazick,* who has brought all of this down on my papa," Anastasia proclaimed.

"Who?" I asked.

"Ida, Ida Dzugash, the whore!"

"Don't be so sure of that, Ani. Some people feel there are other forces at work here."

"Then why has she run away? Why is she gone? He needs her!"

"I don't know, Ani. It could be that her husband's finally caught up to her."

"And what? Kidnapped her?"

Suddenly, Anastasia's English became so muddled and heavily accented that I could hardly understand her, just like when she had called me about her father's missing person status at the airport during the final four Arizona-OSU basket ball game. She ranted, "Americans, dey are too laid back. Dey take nothing seriously enough. Dey can't understand gravity of important situations. And, zheir obsession vit guns will eventually make the shooting of my father tolerable to them, as if just another everyday occurrence to be expected. Democracy—it is hoax! It puts material well-being ahead of human rights...indeed, in zis country, only real human right is right to material well-being if you can get it for yourself. Finer things don't matter."

"Ani, Ani," I pleaded, trying to calm her. "We will find out who shot your father and why. Our system will work. You'll see."

"And what, when you find out?" she complained. "A slap on wrist to criminal? A four-month long trial that frees shooter on a technicality? Humph!"

I gave up trying to calm her down, but I pledged that tomorrow I would go to the police station and tell them everything I thought might have a bearing on the shooting. After all, Art Malone was apparently paying me to do this. And there was plenty to tell. Igor was a manic-depressive refugee from Communist Russia. After being warned not to take a job as maestro of the Columbus Symphony by someone unknown, he had absconded with the wife of one Joseph Dzugash of Chicago to do precisely that. The symphony's former director had attempted to prevent him from taking over the orchestra, but Igor had won this struggle when the former director suffered an embarrassing public rejection by the orchestra's players.

I decided to start at the Columbus PD with Jerry Shapiro, the cop who had the beat my office was on. Jerry was an ok guy, but he couldn't curb his mouth when it came to police work. He spread every rumor he heard, and he was constantly theorizing about things that were none of his business. I was banking on that. I could be sure that if I told him something, no matter how off-base it was, sooner or later he'd pass it along at the station, trying to get in on the department's bigger cases whenever he could.

"So Jerry," I said, casually when he answered his phone, "I was wondering if the department had any information on where Ida Dzugash might have gone. Rosanne and I went over to see her after Igor Bashenko got shot, and it looked liked she'd quickly pulled up stakes and left town."

"Who's Ida Dzugash, counselor?"

"Oh, I thought you knew. She was Igor Bashenko's squeeze. He'd talked her into leaving her husband in

Chicago and coming to Columbus with him. He's been asking for her at the hospital."

"You serious, counselor? I don't think anybody down here knows anything about an Ida Dzugash. You think she's involved?"

"Now, I didn't say that Jerry. The detective work's up to you guys."

CHAPTER THIRTEEN

"It was insulin, fast acting insulin," Detective Picard allowed. Picard was the lead homicide detective at the Columbus PD, a quiet unassuming but often disarming little man who wore a trench coat even in the summertime. When I went to the police station to do Art Malone's bidding and tell them all I knew about the behind-the-scenes politics going on at the symphony board, we got off the subject, and on to my other case, the defense of Ron Herimus for the death of Bruge Biliuss.

"You mean that was insulin in the syringe the police found in the spray booth, not some form of Erythropoietin to illegally raise his red blood cell count or an illegal version of a super anabolic steroid?"

"That's correct," said Picard, being careful not to answer with more information than he was asked for.

I was astounded. "Bruge Biliuss was a diabetic?" I asked. "Well why then have you arrested my—"

"Nope." Picard cut in.

"—client?"

"We arrested him because his fingerprints were all over the syringe," the prosecutor interrupted as she barged in. "I think we're going to terminate this little conversation right now before it becomes a 'discovery session' for defense counsel. Oh, and by the way Mr. Barchrist, you can take what Detective Picard just said, that he wasn't diabetic, with a grain of salt. We really don't know conclusively if Biliuss was or wasn't a diabetic. We're still awaiting his medical records from Belgium."

I walked out of the police station knowing in my heart that Biliuss wasn't diabetic. Picard had slipped up. They were just trying to hide the fact that Biliuss wasn't diabetic, but Picard had probably already checked it out to his satisfaction. He just didn't have the man's medical records from Belgium in his hands yet, but he knew. The prosecutor probably just wanted to spring this news on me at the trial when I didn't have the time to properly react. That way, it would look like Ron Herimus had poisoned Biliuss by injecting him with insulin when he wasn't diabetic, giving him insulin shock, so to speak.

There were a lot of unanswered questions in my mind. Could fast acting insulin kill a non-diabetic? In any event, what were Ronnie's fingerprints doing on that syringe? I called Marinda and asked her to research what happens if you give insulin to someone who is not diabetic. I called Ronnie Herimus and asked if he knew Bruge Biliuss was not a diabetic.

"Why would you ask a thing like that, boss? How would I know or care whether he was diabetic or not?"

"Well, do you know anything about insulin, Ron?"

"Not a thing," he replied. "I give your cat insulin every other day but I don't know anything about it."

Oh, my god, I thought. That's right. Sachmo was an insulin diabetic. That meant Ronnie had easy access to insulin while he was watching my cat. I was the one who ordered it, and I left it with Ron in batches of ten disposable, insulin-filled syringes per box. The facts were getting worse and worse for Ronnie every time I turned around. I also knew that the prosecutor, who was a female, wasn't particularly keen on my friend Ron to begin with. Somewhere in the past there had been some kind of liaison between them. I didn't know what it was all about, but I knew she had a motor cycle, and that outside the boundaries of the legal profession and all its proprieties, she wasn't the prim lawyer she appeared to be today in her blue, straight-cut skirt and suit jacket with her black heels. She rode with the Madras Bulls and so did Ron sometimes.

I decided to have a look at the syringe. So I walked down to the police evidence room and put in a request to see it, but they wouldn't show it to me unless the prosecutor was present. I waited two hours for her to show up, and when she did, she was not happy about having to come down to the police station.

"You're really not saving up your brownie points for the plea bargain phase, are you, Barchrist," she grumped.

"Are we at that stage?" I asked.

"Hell, no!"

"Will we ever be?"

She just creased her lips and grunted, making it clear she thought I had no idea what I was doing.

They brought out the syringe, and I examined it through the clear plastic bag surrounding it. It looked just like the syringes I bought for Sachmo. I examined the glass casing for signs of a batch number. Ah, there it was embossed lightly in the glass. I waited for the prosecutor to divert her attention, and then I took down the number.

When I got back to the office, Marinda was ready with her research on insulin. She had learned that if insulin is injected into a non-diabetic, the result would be a lowering of the blood sugar to a dangerous level shortly after the injection that could induce a coma or seizures. The only way to compensate would be to greatly increase the body's carbohydrate intake immediately. Then came the shocker. Bodybuilders take insulin when they're trying to help their muscles grow because the more carbohydrates they can get their bodies to absorb, the more they'll grow. Many bodybuilders have had really bad low sugar incidents from not exactly covering the insulin units taken with the correct number of carbohydrates. In those cases, the overdose was fatal.

I called Sachmo's vet to ask if the amount of fast-acting insulin in one of his syringes could be fatal if injected into an adult human. The answer was, of course, "It depends." Then I drove over to Ronnie's to see if the batch number I'd taken off the syringe in the police evidence room was the same as the batch of syringes I'd left him for my cat.

It was. It was also time for a heart to heart with my client...cannons of ethics and potential disbarment proceedings, be damned.

"Ron, my friend," I began, "I want you to tell me everything you do with Sachmo's insulin from the time I bring it to you to the time you give it to him, and what you do with the used syringes after you're done."

"Look, boss, let's quit playing these silly games. You believe I took one of Sachmo's syringes over to the spray booth Bruge Biliuss was using down at Vets Memorial and injected him with it. Don't you? Well, if that's what you believe, then maybe you're right. Maybe I should get myself another lawyer."

"No, I don't believe that, Ronnie, but I do think we're at the place where the rubber is hitting the road in this case now, and that if you don't answer my questions completely, there's no way you're not going to do some pretty big time as a guest of the State of Ohio in one of its 'Club Meds' for felons. So PLEASE help me. They think you killed Biliuss by injecting him with insulin when he wasn't a diabetic. An insulin injection has the potential to kill someone who isn't diabetic. They found a syringe with insulin in it and your fingerprints on it next to Biliuss' body in the spray booth. You have access to insulin because I bring it to you for Sachmo. The insulin vial in the police evidence room bears the same batch number on it as the insulin syringes sitting right over there on your counter that I brought you for my cat. I know this because I've been down to the police evidence room and looked at the syringe you...that was found next to Biliuss."

"That I used?"

"What?"

"You almost just said it...the insulin syringe that I used."

"DAMN IT, Ron, will you just answer my questions? Now tell me what you do with these damn things from the time I give them to you to the time you're finished using them."

"OK, I'll tell you, and then I want you to get out of here. If you can't trust me, I'm not going to trust you anymore. I take the syringes out of the box and lay them out on a clean towel on the counter over there so I won't forget to give the shot. When I give Sach a shot, I lay the dirty needle and vial aside on the towel sideways to remind myself that I've given him the shot. Then, I throw it away when I've given him the next one. He gets one shot every other day. Does that satisfy you?"

"You said you had a visitor on the day Biliuss was found dead. Did he come in here to the kitchen?"

"Yes."

"Did he see Sachmo's syringes over there on the counter?"

"He could have. I don't know."

"Did you have any other visitors, here in your kitchen, say a week before that?"

"Mmmm...no, not in the kitchen."

"What was that guy's name, Ron, the guy who came in here to the kitchen?"

Ronnie scratched his head. "I've been thinking about that," he said. "He was really a weird guy. Told me he was sure Biliuss wouldn't win the competition and that I was probably going to, especially if I took their steroids. Biliuss was refusing to take their stuff," he said.

"Can you describe this guy?"

"Very tall; wore a black suit; and his arms were very long, I remember. Also, he had huge hands. I don't know why I noticed those things. His hair was sandy red and straight, and he wore it over to one side, kind of like Hitler."

CHAPTER FOURTEEN

I had just visited Igor Bashenko again in his hospital room at the Wexner Medical Center, where, despite the fluid lines attached to him and the constant pinging of his heart monitor, he was waxing triumphant because the doctors had declared the bullet had not affected any of his major organs or tissues. A huge white bandage, reinforced with surgical tape, circling around his upper torso, clung to his body, as if his right shoulder and arm might fall off without it.

"I shall live to direct another day," Igor declared, "just perhaps something not quite as realistic as the *1812 Overture* with its dangerous pyrotechnics." Everyone in the room offered a gratuitous laugh, although the fear and worry in Anastasia's eyes remained palpable.

"In Russia, they would have posted a guard at the door of such a notable as my papa, who was shot like this for no reason," she complained.

I tried to calm her once again, but now, I had to leave for another mission, this time at the King Avenue Coroner's Office, which was just four short blocks from the hospital. There, a different story was unfolding.

Nobody was in the morgue when I arrived, not even in the front office, which gave me the opportunity to disguise myself by slipping into some scrubs and putting a mask over my face so I could enter without any authority to do so. On the gurney, with a toe tag dangling from the right foot was a body covered by a white sheet, a blue pattern sewn through it, repeating the emblem of the Franklin County Sheriff's Office. It was Bruge Biliuss. The tag revealed more than I'd learned to date about the unfortunate corpse: "Bruge Christotum Biliuss, married, no children, 27 years of age, number 54A Avenue du Astrolebe, Lissewege, Belgium.   Occupation: research   assistant, pharmaceuticals."

As I stood there waiting for the Medical Examiner, Officer Shapiro entered the antiseptic white tile room wearing a surgical smock two sizes too large for him and a paper hat that made him look like a French baker. He was followed by the serious-faced detective, Anthony Picard. The Medical Examiner, an eager-looking young fellow named Dr. Butsko, was a recent graduate of the Ohio State School of Medicine. As an undergraduate he had majored in Criminology. He entered through a side door, and didn't seem to notice me. Nobody asked who I was and I volunteered nothing. The M.E. whipped the cover off Biliuss' torso with a flare. There he was lying on a steel table, like a recently cleaned fish, organs neatly arrayed in separate pans to one side of him. It was all very clinical, no putrid smells, no fluids oozing from the body, no blood or smashed bones...just an empty chest cavity with muscular legs at one end and an inanimate face at the other.

Dr. Butsko began slicing away around the neck area while cheerfully spitting a storm of medical jargon into an overhead microphone. *Five more years at this job,* I thought to myself, *and a strong dose of reality will have stripped this guy's sophomoric veneer away and taught him the gravity and respect with which he should be approaching the body of someone who has passed away.* Now the M.E. was cutting the subject's facial skin with little scraping motions and peeling it away in flaps and clamping them back. Then he began filleting the muscular neck tissues. The cuts made a crackling sound which obviously disturbed Officer Shapiro to the point where he complained uncomfortably, "I don't see how all this cutting and scraping is going to determine whether this man died of insulin shock."

"Ah, that question falls under the purview of the toxicology lab, and the answer will not be known for about two weeks," Butsko responded. "It's not part of my job. My job is just to slice and dice," he stated blithely, returning to his work.

Just then some sort of fluid squirted from the neck of the corpse, and Shapiro, his hands pressed against his mouth, ran off looking for a waste basket in which to throw up. Picard's eyes looked up, regarding him disgustedly, although his face remained in the direction of the body on the table.

"Hmm," said the M.E. "Look, a broken hyoid bone...no, make that a *shattered* hyoid bone," he said, directing his comments toward the microphone. "The lungs were purple, and this just confirms what I've been thinking all along."

"I believe you, Doc," Shapiro coughed, his eyes averted.

The M.E. smiled broadly. "First autopsy, eh?"

"Of course not," Shapiro lied.

"Sometimes they can get a little messy," continued the M.E.

"So he was strangled then?" Picard asked, incredulously, ignoring Shapiro's discomfort.

"Not exactly, this was a little more clinical. Look, there are hardly any bruises on the neck. Whoever did this knew exactly what he was doing...only a student of anatomy could have accomplished it, and that would have been by grabbing this man by the back of the neck ever so lightly with his forefingers, and forcing his thumbs right up against the bone from the front until it snapped. The force was tremendous but very concentrated. Look, there appears to be no other damage about the neck...tracheal rings aren't crushed...cricoid cartilage is still intact. The subject died because of asphyxia associated with pharyngeal spasm, not strangulation as we typically perceive it."

"Whoa, hold up. I don't get it when you start with the medical lingo. You say there are no bruises about the neck, and yet this guy's air supply was cut off. How can that be?" Picard asked.

Dr. Butsco took the opportunity to show off his criminology education. "The hyoid bone is very special," he began. "It's shaped like a horseshoe and it's the only bone in the human body that's not attached to any other bones: rather it is attached to a network of muscles and ligaments which float it directly under the tongue, and its primary role is to support the weight of the tongue, allowing a person to articulate while speaking. When the hyoid bone is broken, the back of the tongue sinks into the air passage and asphyxiation occurs. In cases where we have no tissue to inspect for bruises about the neck and only skeletal remains are presented for autopsy, a broken hyoid bone can seal the deal that the cause of death was either asphyxiation or strangulation. Here, however, since there's no tissue bruising, it was clearly asphyxiation."

Forgetting I had received no authorization to be present at the autopsy, I cleared my throat getting ready to ask a question. The M.E. looked up surprised. "And who might you be?" he asked.

Now, Shapiro paid me back for putting him onto the fact the other day that Ida Dzugash might be a part of the picture in the Igor Bashenko shooting. "He's OK," said the officer. "He's working on this case with us over at the District Attorney's Office. Winston Barchrist."

"Assistant District Attorney Barchrist," the M.E said with a new edge in his voice, "Please identify yourself for the tape recorder, and cover your hair with a scrub hat. You'll find one in that drawer. We don't often get lawyers in here looking over our shoulders." Picard, who was hated by the prosecutor, said nothing, probably because he was glad to see me getting a leg up in the defense of my client.

"I'd be happy too," I replied, thinking that, after all, it was not me, but Shapiro who'd identified me as an Assistant Attorney General. So I couldn't get into any trouble with the D.A. "My name is Winston Barchrist III. May I ask a question, doctor?"

"As long as you don't put me on the witness stand," he cackled with casual nervousness.

"In addition to the profound findings of your examination with which you've just acquainted us, and I assume they will appear in your report as the cause of death, there may also be evidence, when the toxicology report comes back, of insulin shock as a cause of death. I base this on some physical evidence found with the body at the time it was discovered. Understand, I don't doubt your conclusion for a millisecond, but will there be any way to determine which occurred first...the insulin shock, if indeed it occurred, or the broken hyoid bone?"

The M.E. appeared irritated. "Are you saying someone could have administered an overdose of insulin, and thereafter broken the subject's hyoid bone? That's an unlikely redundancy, but if such evidence appears, you can be certain the final coroner's report will deal with it."

"Yes, but can you explain how the question might be disposed of? What procedures will be used?

The M.E. remained silent for a long time. Then he uttered tentatively, as if he was going beyond his depth,

"If the cause of death is asphyxiation, there could be signs of cyanosis. With insulin shock, no signs of cyanosis will appear."

"What is cyanosis? Are there signs of it?" I asked

"Well," announced the M.E., "we're about done here for the time being. I see no reason for me to waste taxpayer's money by speculating on the matter you suggest until I see some evidence of insulin shock."

"In other words," chimed in Shapiro, turning toward me with a sly grin, "you're a lawyer and you'll have to figure that one out for yourself, when and if the time comes up."

CHAPTER FIFTEEN

After the autopsy, I was really confused. Had Bruge Biliuss died of insulin shock or asphyxiation from a broken hyoid? The latter would mean Ronnie was free. But what if both causes of death were evident?

I needed to know more than the cause of death before I could answer that. What was the motive for the killing? Ronnie certainly had none, in my mind, although I knew the police and the prosecutor didn't see it that way. They would think a $5000 prize and a career as a professional body builder were certainly good motives for getting rid of the only person standing in one's way of achieving those goals.

There seemed to be nowhere to turn next in investigating the matter. I had a syringe with Ronnie's fingerprints telling me Ron did it, and Ron telling me he was nowhere near the spray booth where the crime happened. I had detective Picard telling me Bruge wasn't diabetic, so a blast of insulin would have killed him. I had a match between Sachmo's lot of syringes in Ron's kitchen and the syringe found beside the body. I had a very tall nameless man in a black suit with very long arms, big hands and sandy straight red hair in Ron's kitchen, with access to Sachmo's syringes, right before the murder, and I had a broken hyoid bone with no evidence as to who broke it. There was only one thing left to do: find the man with the red hair.

"Actually," said Marinda as I laid this all out for her back at the office, "there's something else you could do: find out more about Bruge Biliuss."

"But that would probably mean a trip to Belgium," I groused.

"Ok, then," she retorted cheerfully. "So let's go." Marinda was always looking for ways to get out of Columbus and travel to interesting places.

"Don't be ridiculous, I can't afford a trip like that, let alone a trip like that for both of us."

"Oh, yes, you can. What about your March Madness winnings?"

"OSU did not win the National Men's Basketball Championship, and besides the money I did win during the tournament is for a vacation to Europe for me and–"

"You would put that in the way of saving your friend Ron Herimus from jail?"

"—Rosanne. I've already told her we're going to Italy!"

"So take her with you to Belgium and then go to Italy. I'll stay here and watch the office, boss, and when you get back, you'll give me a nice long vacation with pay."

"But I don't have enough to go to Belgium and take her with me right now."

"Boss, you've got enough. Just sell your Moped. Remember, you've got a decent car now."

Before I could respond, the phone rang. It was Art Malone wanting to chat. "Did you hear?" he asked excitedly. "Aiden-Life Pharmaceuticals just jumped ten points on the NYEX. They've introduced a new medication that cures Parkinson's disease."

"No, I hadn't heard that. Do you own a lot of Aiden-Life, Art?"

"No, it just really pisses me off that that bastard Heinrich Wabstmann is going to get even richer now. He's already the talk of the town, and now there's a rumor he's going to retire from his CEO post at Aiden so he can run for mayor and throw all his power and influence around, kind of like Michael Bloomberg in New York. He wants to make Columbus the foremost conservative city in the United States."

"Michael Bloomberg's a good mayor, Art. He was duly elected. He didn't get the job just because he's rich."

"Yah, but if Herr Heinrich Wabstmann gets in as mayor, it will be like when Hitler became Chancellor of Germany. He'll use his money to put in the fix. The city council members might think they're going to control him, but they won't be able to. We'll have tax breaks of all kinds for corporations, lousy schools, no city services, and construction projects only for his buddies. You know Herr Wabstmann didn't build Aiden-Life himself. His grandfather did. He just inherited enough stock to get himself elected CEO, that's all. Then, he took the company public to make money for himself and for no other reason, and, you know, until this Parkinson's drug came along, that company was going nowhere under him. He's been too busy being a big wheel on things like the symphony board."

"Well, Art, what can you do? Sometimes the high born just get lucky, I guess."

Art Malone hated Heinrich Wabstmann and Heinrich Wabstmann hated Art Malone. That's just the way it was. Malone was worth almost a billion dollars, but to Wabstmann he was "white trash" not a self-made man who'd risen up from a West Virginia holler to run a huge steel company. The only reason Wabstmann had put him on the symphony board was to get at his money. Wabstmann saw himself as an unstoppable fund raising dynamo with the power to do anything that might extract money from rich people for the causes he supported.

Malone, on the other hand, didn't give a hoot about Igor Bashenko's musical capabilities. He just wanted him to be the leader of the Columbus Symphony Orchestra because Wabstmann didn't, and Wabstmann needed to be put in his place. Wabstmann knew music and was intrigued by Vadea's musical background. Malone didn't know a G clef from a Bass clef.

Wabstmann had a deep interest in his man, Janic Vadea, perhaps because he was cultured and European in background. The two men also seemed to be fast friends socially, as well as associates, professionally, Wabstmann having been Vadea's guest at his family castle outside Belgrade, where the two men rode horses together and played chess.

It took at least fifteen minutes to extract myself from Malone's telephone tirade against Wabstmann, but I tried to be patient, knowing all along that I had a lot of work to do on the Herimus case and that I didn't know where to start. Rich people deserve as much patience as poor people, I guess, so I listened to Art Malone politely.

Marinda brought in a list of the companies that were vendors at the Schwarzenegger Classic. There were five drug sales outfits, and it was going to take quite a while to check out all of them for an employee fitting the description of the man Ronnie told me had visited him in his kitchen on the day of the Biliuss murder, but it was either that or go to Belgium to check out Biliuss himself. Ron said the stranger in his kitchen was pushing him to take his company's steroids. Therefore, I could cut down the size of this job by determining which of these companies sold steroid products. Trudy Fischel would be of help to me there with her computer snooping capabilities.

"So, you're thinking of taking steroids now, aye, big guy?" she quipped. "What's the matter? Rosanne doesn't think you're cut enough as is? Or is it that you've developed back problems from laying around on your couch all day?"

"Very funny, Trudy, but, no, this is for a case I'm working on—Ronnie Herimus' case."

"You're defending him?"

"Right, if not me, then who? You know he hasn't got any money to pay a lawyer."

"You mean to pay a real criminal lawyer."

"That's very funny too, Trudy."

"Take it easy there, big guy. I just like to throw a few barbs your way when I can. Actually, since this is for Ronnie, there'll be no charge for my services. Oh, and as far as Rosanne's concerned, I was just kidding there too. If she doesn't like your muscles the way they are, you know I'd be glad to take over for her any time. I like big men."

Even though she often called me fat, Trudy had made it very clear for a long time that she was available for any romantic dalliance I might want, "or need," and she was never going to stop trying, Rosanne or no Rosanne. Rosanne didn't like her much, because she had a really bad reputation in Bexley involving the husbands of other women. Needless to say, when it came to my business dealings with Trudy, I kept them as secret as possible from Rosanne.

CHAPTER SIXTEEN

Joseph Dzugash turned out to be nobody to mess with. A small arms manufacturer's rep, he showed up in Columbus with his conceal and carry permit, a Magnum .357 in his shoulder holster, and a Smith & Wesson .380 Bodyguard strapped to his ankle; and he had no compunction about openly brandishing these armaments when he paid a surprise visit to Anastasia and Picup at their home. He had a huge build, like a bear, and with his stature and his weapons he cut an alarming figure.

Joseph missed his wife Ida a lot when he finally arrived back in Chicago from Europe. Not only was she gone, but so were her clothes, her harp and $25,000 from their joint savings account. There were no wiring instructions for the money. She had simply withdrawn it in cash. There were also persistent rumors in the neighborhood that Igor Bashenko, known to many at the time as the Director of the Trans-Siberian Orchestra, had been seen going in and out of the Dzugash home while Joseph was gone. Then Joseph found a bill of lading for the shipment of Ida's harp to a Columbus freight forwarder in Ida's drawer in their Rogers Park home. So he retained the Milo-Grogan Detective Agency in Columbus to help him locate Ida.

There were plenty of publicity posters plastered around town depicting Igor Bashenko in tails and tux waiving a baton determinedly from his dais in front of the orchestra, but no publicity shots or newspaper photographs showing him with Ida. The Milo-Grogan

Detective Agency kept two special photos of her on their bulletin board at the office, one frontal and one side view, which Joseph had sent along shortly after hiring them. They looked more like mug shots than like the exotic Ida Dzugash. Joseph also mentioned that Igor Bashenko might somehow be involved according to the rumors he was hearing in Chicago, but the people at Milo-Grogan were having no luck finding her.

Then, one evening an off-duty Milo-Grogan agent fortuitously tried to pick Ida up while sitting at one of the bars she frequented during the nights Igor was at orchestra practice or out for the evening with concertmaster Miriam Jaspers—going over scores the orchestra was performing. After a few drinks, Ida began running off at the mouth about her relationship with the orchestra director, which tipped off the private eye that he might have located Dzugash's prey. Ida ranted on and on about how, at first, Bashenko had seemed so exciting, but gradually had become a bore, and about how much she disliked Bashenko's daughter who had brought the two of them to Columbus via a limousine service she owned.

The agency alerted Joseph, and he immediately flew to Columbus to reclaim his wife. He could have done so at the orchestra's premier concert, which ticket purchase records later revealed he had attended. But, as he explained it, he chose not to approach Ida publicly at that time because it might have created a scene. Then, after the surprise shooting at the concert, Ida was nowhere to be found. So Joseph dropped in on the Andropovs to attempt to threaten them into telling him where she was.

Anastasia was so afraid of him that she excused herself and called me from her kitchen, whispering to come right over and to bring the police. When I showed up, Officer Shapiro was waiting outside in his cruiser.

Dzugash was in their tiny living room with his jacket flap pulled back revealing the butt end of his huge Magnum .357, and Picup was cowering behind his wife.

"Yes, Mr. Dzugash," Anastasia whimpered. "Very true. We brought your vife to Columbus in our limo with Igor Bashenko, but it vas not, like you say, 'kidnapping.'"

"No, it was more like a sex crime," Picup chimed in from behind his wife, "Bashenko, he is maniac, sex maniac, like Rasputin; he seduces women."

"Picup, please!" Ani screamed. "You were not even there." Then she turned to Dzugash, protesting, "Ve don't know where your wife is, and my Papa, he is in hospital." Dzugash began explaining to them that he was very sorry Igor Bashenko was in the hospital, but he was going to put holes the size of grapes into their black Chrysler limousine with his .357 if they didn't reveal where Ida was hiding.

"I don't think you want to do that, Mr. Dzugash," I said as I walked in. "The police are right outside. This is Columbus, Ohio, not Chicago."

"These people have already told me they drove my Ida back here with that Bashenko. You know what that is? That's kidnapping."

"Only if she didn't come willingly, sir, and she did."

"And who might you be?" Dzugash demanded.

"I'm Winston Barchrist III, the Andropov's lawyer, and I was present throughout the trip back to Columbus."

A confused look gripped Dzugash's face. He moved over to the worn couch and slumped into it without any invitation to sit down. His eyes were like tight, dark beads below his black, bushy eyebrows. He smoothed his thick, dark hair with a huge hand, and then he felt the bottom of his black, heavily-waxed mustache with his finger tips. It was as if someone had extracted steel from his spine. He began breathing heavily. The .038 peeked out from under his pant cuff when he sat down.

"Bie chodishe bebier? (You want a drink?),"* Anastasia asked.

"Moshet buiet vodka, spasebo, (Perhaps Vodka, thank you),"* he whispered in his native Russian, taking on the demeanor of someone who had been conquered. "Did she come willingly to Columbus with this musician?" he asked.

It was obvious that Dzugash, after all his years of marriage, knew enough about his wife to believe what I had said, but that he didn't want to face it. European men of his age were very hard on their women. They expected complete subservience.

"I will kill her when I find her."

Just then, Jerry Shapiro poked his head through the door and walked in. "And, what about Igor Bashenko, Mr. Dzugash? Do you feel the same way about him?" Shapiro asked.

Then he turned to me. "Thanks, counselor, for the little tip you gave me about this Ida Dzugash the other day. It looks like it's turning out to be our first break in the symphony shooting. Now, I'm going to ask Mr. Dzugash here to come down to the station with me to answer a few questions. I hope you'll come voluntarily, Mr. Dzugash. If not, I could always arrest you for "menacing" with these two fine guns of yours and your threat to turn the Andropov limousine into Swiss cheese with them. Do you wish to come voluntarily, or shall I call for back-up?" With that, he unsnapped the leather pouch on his black belt that held his handcuffs.

Dzugash looked like he had suddenly been transformed from a Russian bear into a bear rug, as he arose and preceded Shapiro out the front door voluntarily. Shapiro didn't bother to use the cuffs.

"You want to come down to the station with us too, counselor, just to see what's going on?"

"Thanks for the invite, Jerry," I replied, "but I think I'll leave the examination of Mr. Dzugash in your capable hands. I've got another case I need to work on right now."

"And would that be the Herimus case, counselor?" Shapiro inquired.

"It might be."

"Well, you're right counselor. You better get crackin' on that one. The prosecutor's getting ready to go to the Grand Jury with it any day now."

When I got back to my office, there was a report waiting for me on my desk that Marinda had taken over the phone from Trudy. All of the pharmaceutical companies at the Schwarzenegger Fitness Classic sold steroids. Some of them had up to one hundred fifteen salesmen. Notably, one of the companies, Pharmea Bruxelles, was a subsidiary of Aiden-Life Pharmaceuticals, Heinrich Wabstmann's company. No employee names were available, and, of course, there were no descriptions of the companies' sales people. This was a blind alley. I'd never be able to pinpoint the man who visited Ron Herimus in his kitchen on the day of the murder using this information.

Next to the report was a flight itinerary to Brussels with a note from Marinda..."Do you want me to get a ticket for Rosanne too, Boss?" Marinda was no dummy. She knew the only thing I could do now was try to find out more about who Bruge Biliuss was.

CHAPTER SEVENTEEN

Rosanne slept peacefully with her head against the bulkhead near the window with the shade down. The sun was just beginning to come up. Crammed into a middle seat next to her, the only parts of my three-hundred-pound body that were asleep were my feet. The flight to Belgium was eight hours and 40 minutes from JFK to Brussels. Lissewege, home of what was left of the Biliuss family, which now consisted only of Geertje Biliuss, Bruge's wife, is a village outside Bruges in Western Flanders, the Dutch speaking part of Belgium. Obviously, Bruge Biliuss was named after the city of Bruges. Lissewege is 108 kilometers from Brussels by car or train. So, our plan was to spend two days and two nights in Brussels recovering from the travel and being tourists, and then proceed to Lisswege to look up Geertje. Near Lissewege, we would get a hotel room in Bruges, a medieval city which, itself, is one of the country's biggest tourist attractions. We had given up on combining the trip with a visit to Rome, and were now contenting ourselves with touring the Benelux counties.

In the back of the plane, a steady murmur began. I looked over my seatback at a group of men in black hats with prayer shawls loosely draped over dark suits and phylacteries, draping their foreheads and wound around their exposed right arms. As they chanted, they bent at the waist and swayed from side to side like "Shakers." Rabbi Billy had given me a heads up about this before we left. Antwerp, Belgium, the home of the world's largest diamond exchange, was also the home of one of the most fervent Orthodox Jewish communities in the world. Thus, I should expect to see men *dovening* their morning prayers in the back of the plane as we approached Brussels International Airport at sun up. I touched Rosanne gently, directing her attention to the minion back by the restrooms. According to Billy, it was an unusual sight, except on El Al jets approaching Israel in the morning.

"Yich," Rosanne said, screwing up her face. "Think of all that halitosis." Then she laughed. "Just kidding, I know how upset you get when I make fun of my own people. If you ever convert, you can do that too. Won't that be fun?" She smiled coyly.

"Why would I ever want to convert, Rosanne?"

That was a mistake which ended our conversation abruptly. Luckily, just then the cabin attendant leaned over me with our breakfasts. The paltry meal seemed more like breakfast hors d'oeuvres than breakfast itself—only two eggs, three sausages, home fries, two pieces of toast, juice and coffee. I was starving after last night's so-called dinner and this was hardly enough food for a man of my girth. The only second servings one could expect from the parsimonious KLM Airline were further cups of coffee.

So, I contented myself with looking out the window as the plane dropped altitude on its approach to Brussels. The most impressive things about the little country's topography along its 30- mile-deep coastal region were the sand dunes, the flat pasture lands and the polders or land reclaimed from the sea and protected by dikes. Gradually, the scene gave way to a rolling central plain, and then below us spread Brussels, the capital of Belgium, and the *de facto* capital of the European Union. The city is bi-lingual: its Flemish people speaking Dutch, and its Walloons speaking

French. It was founded in the tenth century by Charlemagne, and it is very historic. All I could think of doing after we landed, however, was getting my hands on one of its famed Belgian waffles.

We checked into the *Citadines Brussels Ste. Catherine,* a hotel in the heart of the city, and Rosanne immediately dragged me out to look at the city's flower market. It could have been worse, however, because only one street over, the Avenue Louise was located, lined with its world class shops. Luckily, she didn't notice it. As for me, I was just looking for a real Belgian waffle. When we returned to the hotel, I made arrangements through the concierge for train tickets to Bruges the day after next. In Bruges, I planned to rent a car.

I then checked with the front desk to see whether they had any telephone directories for Lissewege, but I couldn't understand the clerk's response because, like the Dutch, the Flemish spoke English from the back of their mouths, gutturally, mumbling the words in their throats and swallowing them. Rosanne had better luck speaking French with the man. She came back with the phonebook for the entire West Flanders province.

"He says to look under Bruges if we can't find Geertje or Bruge Biliuss in the Lissewege section," she said.

Leafing through the Lissewege section of the book, there it was—Biliuss, Geertje/Bruge. I dialed the number, hoping to set up an appointment with Geertje. A low female voice answered, that I didn't understand.

"Geertje Biliuss? I asked.

"Ja? Goede Avond?"

"My name is Winston Barchrist and I'm investigating the death of—"

"Ik versta net niet."

—your husband, Bruge."

"Bruge? Ik verst net niet."

"I don't think she understands English," I said, turning to Rosanne.

"Here, let me try," she said, taking the phone. *"Parlez-vous francais,* Geertje?"

"Nee."

"We're going to need an interpreter," Rosanne said, turning to me. "See if you can get the desk clerk to help us."

After an extensive conversation with Rosanne in French, the desk clerk spoke into the phone to Geertje in Dutch telling her who we were, what we wanted to do, and trying to set up an appointment for us with her. Then he began shaking his head negatively and telling Rosanne in French that Geertje would not meet with us.

"Pouquoi pas?" Rosanne asked the clerk. He then embarked on a long conversation in Dutch with Geertje, after which he explained that too many people from her husband's company had been coming around disturbing her about her husband's death and telling her not to talk to anybody about it if she wants to collect her husband's company life insurance.

"Well, we can't afford another dead end," I told Rosanne, "especially after coming all this way. Ask him to ask her what the name of the company is."

The clerk followed Rosanne's instruction and reported back that the company's name was *Pharmae Bruxelles,* Ltd. The name had no meaning to me as pronounced with the desk clerk's French accent, so Rosanne had him write it down. What I saw when he handed me the slip of paper with the name on it was a complete surprise.

"Rosanne, this is a subsidiary of Aiden-Life, the American company headquartered in Columbus run by Heinrich Wabstmann! The company was one of those at the Schwarzenegger Classic selling steroids to participants and generally advertising its products. But there's something very strange here that I must think about. I'll have to check my notes, but Ronnie told me that on the day of Biliuss' death, someone visited him, someone from a company that had a name he couldn't remember—some sort of pharmacy company.

"He couldn't remember the full name. Ronnie said that person told him Biliuss was not taking that company's steroid, and so if Ronnie took it and won the competition, he'd get a nice endorsement contract from the company. That company may actually have been Pharmae Bruxelles. I know this because the only company working the Schwarzenegger Classic that Marinda found to contain the name "Pharmae" in it was this company...Pharmae Bruxelles, Ltd., and Ronnie remembered it as a pharmacy company. If Biliuss worked for this company, why wouldn't he have been taking its steroid.?"

CHAPTER EIGHTEEN

Proceeding under the rubric, "Half of success is persistence," we decided to go to Lissewege even though Geertje said she would not welcome us. Lissewege is a peaceful little village of white-chalked houses with orange-tile roofs protected by dikes, and commanded by a gigantic church with a spire 150 feet high, the building of which was overseen by the Knights Templar between 1230 and 1270. Today, the town is an artist's colony, among other things. We hired an interpreter in Bruges and drove the 10 kilometers from there to Lissewege in a rented Renault Twingo, which we soon took to calling our Renault *Merd,* because we couldn't figure out how to back it up. It was a very uncomfortable car for me. In the back seat, next to our interpreter, a young woman of 28, was a basket filled with baguettes, cheeses, pastry cakes and a bottle of wine, all to be given to Geertje if she let us in.

Our interpreter led the way to Geertje's door, while we lagged safely behind, holding the huge gift basket. Her house was on a beautiful canal that ran all the way from Bruges to Lissewege. She greeted the interpreter reluctantly. Geertje Biliuss was a very pretty Flemish women dressed in a peasant style skirt and a blouse with draw-strings across a V-neckline, who looked like she hadn't smiled in days. Her long, reddish-brown hair was pinned up into a white, hooded bonnet, and she was holding a Cheshire cat. What seemed like an endless colloquy in Dutch ensued between her and our interpreter, which ended as the interpreter stepped back, gestured and introduced us as *Meneer* Barchrist und *Frauen* Harmon. A thin smile appeared on Geertje's lips as she cast her eyes on the gift basket and nodded almost furtively.

"Kom hier," she gestured, opening the door wider and stepping aside so we could enter.

"Dank u wel," replied the interpreter.

"What did you say to get her to let us in?" I asked.

"I told her you were a lawyer from the United States who could help her, and that you had come a long way to see her because the people who run the Schwarzenegger Festival were very sad about what happened to her husband. I also told her that Frauen Harmon was an accountant who knew well the value of the damages that had occurred. Is all this not true?"

"It's true, but it's not really why we're here," Rosanne said.

"Well," said the interpreter, "let us go in and see what happens."

Inside, we had tea, and Geertje warmed up fast. She worked as an administrative worker at the *Stadhuis*, or city hall on the *Burg*, or town square in Bruges. She told us her husband Bruge had been a research assistant for Pharmae Bruxelles, Ltd., located near Bruges for seven years. For most of his tenure he had worked on a project called NSTC involving the development of a substance for the American market to cure Parkinson's disease without the use of stem cell therapy, which had become so highly politicized in the United States.

A long discussion in Dutch followed, after which the interpreter smiled, explaining that the leader of Bruge's company was steadfastly against stem cell research because he was very conservative. I asked who the leader was, and she answered, *"Herr* Heinrich Wabstmann of the United States." The answer startled me. So it was true. Bruge Biliuss was an employee of

Heinrich Wabstmann, the nemesis of Igor Bashenko in another world. Hmp!

The drug, Ragasiline, that Bruge had worked on was now being manufactured in Europe for sale by the parent company, Aiden-Life, in the United States. Bruge was asked to sign a contract agreeing never to divulge its contents, or anything else about the new drug, as were all of the research assistants who worked on it.

"How did Bruge happen to come to Columbus for the Arnold Schwarzenegger Classic?" I asked.

"The company knew of his interest in body building," Geertje explained. She said that he had won many amateur contests in the Netherlands, Belgium and France, and as a reward for his services to Pharmae Bruxelles, the company paid to send him to the Schwarzenegger Classic in Columbus, where he had a chance of winning a contest that would lead to his becoming a professional. Pharmae Bruxelle would then give him an endorsement contract for the human growth hormone produced by the company that he was using in Columbus. It was to be a sort of bonus for him.

"That's very generous," I replied, but when Geertje told us this, it ran a "red flag" up the pole for me again. Hadn't the company's representative told Ron Herimus that Bruge Biliuss *was refusing* to use the company's steroid, if indeed, the company involved was Pharmae Bruxelles? This had to be checked out.

"Ask her if she ever saw Bruge take the steroid manufactured by the company," I told our interpreter. With that, a short repartee in Dutch ensued, with Geertje smiling as she answered, "Ja, ja, ja...Oh, ja."

"Oh, yes," answered the interpreter. "She would even make sure he took it in the mornings before he was out of bed. She loved his big muscles." The three women in the room giggled.

"What's so funny about that, Rosanne?" I asked.

"Oh, nothing," she said absent mindedly.

"Well, I think it's a very important piece of information in this case. It may mean that someone was trying to set up Ronnie Herimus if it's true, because Ronnie was told the exact opposite by a visitor he had on the day of Bruge's death."

"It may also mean that someone liked her husband's big muscles in the morning before he got out of bed," Rosanne laughed.

"Well, that's not very germane to the case, Rosanne."

"Sure it is. It means they liked each other."

"Well, I think we need to know other things, like was Bruge diabetic? Did he have any heart problems?"

The interpreter translated and Geertje came back with negative answers to both questions.

"Well, let me see if I have anything else? Oh, yes, did Bruge have any problems at work...any problems with his job?"

Geertje's face turned ashen for a moment, and she looked away, giving no answer.

"Well, can you give me the names of some of his friends or fellow workers at Pharmae Bruxelles?"

It seemed like the interpreter had to coax this information out of Geertje, telling her not to worry, that it would be ok. Finally, Geertje revealed some names: Niels Blenker, Hans van Kugee and Felix de Wolff. But she insisted that if we interviewed any of these people, we should not to talk to them at the Pharmae Bruxelles business office.

A little over an hour had passed, and by that time, I had consumed most of the pastries that came in the basket we brought Geertje. But the breads, cheeses and wines were all still intact. It was time to leave.

As I was pouring myself back into our little rented Renault *Merd,* outside Geertje's house, I noticed something strange, but I didn't give it much thought. When we had arrived, there was a man with red hair standing across the canal in an alcove with a bicycle. Surprisingly, now that we were leaving, he was still there, over an hour later, as if he was watching Geertje's house.

Things had actually gone well enough with Geertje so that she and Rosanne hugged good-by when we left. When the man across the canal saw this, he mounted his bike and followed us down the other side of the canal, looking over the waterway at our car from time to time. Finally, a barge passed between us, and I lost him, or he lost us, I don't know which.

Back in Bruges, the call light was flicking on the phone in the hotel room. Igor Bashenko had convinced Marinda to let him know how to contact me. The hospital had released him, and he was continuing his recovery at home. He was expecting to return to his duties as maestro in two weeks but he was scared.

"I want to thank you for putting that animal, Joseph Dzugash, into the hands of the police, Winston," he said. "It probably saved my life, but as I talk to you today, my friend, I'm still living in fear. Very strange things are happening, and I think someone may be trying to finish the job on me. I may need your help as a lawyer...

"You know Dzugash was under suspicion as being the shooter, but then something very strange happened. Ida came forward and gave the police a sworn statement that she didn't come willingly to Columbus from her home in Chicago. She says I forced her to come, and that she wanted to stay home and wait for her husband to get back from Europe. She also swore that on the night of the first concert of the season,

Joseph Dzugash was in town, because a private detective he had hired found her in Columbus; that Joseph sought her out at the Ohio Theater; and, that the two of them left and spent the evening together in an upscale restaurant on the second floor of the Verne Riffe Office Tower around the corner. Joseph didn't have a gun with him that night according to her. She said that she spent their time together at that restaurant explaining how she had come to Columbus with me and how I was keeping her captive here."

"That's ridiculous! All that is ridiculous! I'm sure there's nobody who can corroborate that story. It's an outright lie," I assured Igor.

"According to the police, there is someone who can corroborate it."

"Who?"

"The police won't reveal the name of the witness."

"Well, when I get home, we'll get all of this straightened out. I was there when we brought Ida to Columbus! I rode home from Chicago to Columbus in the Andropov limo with Ida and Anastasia. On the night of the concert, I know Ida was in the Palace Theater sitting alone in a box because I saw her there."

"I hope we can get it straightened out, my friend. I hope so. The police are keeping a lid on the trouble I'm in with Dzugash right now, but the thing is, I think I may be in a little trouble with them too, for unlawful abduction or something like that. I don't know whether you knew this or not but Ida and I had been fighting for a long time like cats and dogs. She hated Columbus. She hated our condo, and she accused me of ignoring her, even cheating on her. It got so bad she said she hated me too. I think she and Joseph may be planning to sue me. So, as you can see, Winston, I really need your help."

"I will help you, my friend," I said, "as soon as I get back to Columbus."

"It will be good if you can, Winston. I know it was morally wrong of me to pursue another man's wife, and I am sorry I ever did it, but somehow I couldn't stop myself. Now I'm being punished heavily for it. I've been shot. I'm afraid something else bad may happen to me, and I'm very confused. I have a season with the orchestra to finish out, and I don't know if I can do it with all that's going on. I need your help."

"I'll call you as soon as I get back," I promised.

CHAPTER NINETEEN

That night Rosanne and I went out on the town. We sat at a table in the Market Square, drinking cappuccinos and looking up at the Bruges Belfort, a medieval bell tower bathed in spotlights that dominates the square in the city's center.

"It's beautiful, isn't it?" a voice from behind us said. "You know, it's over 83 meters tall, and there are 366 stairs to the top. It was built in the year 1240, and it used to be taller, but three times fires have burnt down the spires that have topped it off. Today, it has 47 bells inside."

"Are you a tour guide?" Rosanne asked.

"No, I just live in Bruges."

"But your English is perfect, without a trace of a Flemish or any Walloon accent."

"Oh, I'm Flemish by birth, but my English is like yours because I grew up in the States."

The man behind us was tall with sandy-red hair and a distorted look to his posture. His arms were too long for his body and he had a large pronounced head and face. Strikingly, his smile revealed a gold eye-tooth that flashed when his lips parted. He was wearing a blue blazer over a navy and white, striped jersey with khakis. Had he had the right cap, he might have looked like a sailor in the Belgian Navy, if they had a navy.

"May I join you?" he inquired.

"Yes, please do," Rosanne said, as the man placed his mug of beer on our table and pulled up his chair. He held out his hand to shake mine, announcing his name—"Rolph Van Heyde. Where are you from in the States?"

"I'm Winston Barchrist and this is Rosanne Harmon; we're from Columbus, Ohio," I replied.

"Never been there," Rolph offered. "What brings you to Bruges? We don't get that many non-European tourists here, especially from Iowa."

"We're from Ohio, not Iowa," Rosanne corrected, "and we're on a vacation, but it's actually business that has sidelined us for a few days to Bruges." Then she got downright blabby. "We came here for a meeting."

I reached under the table and squeezed her knee, trying to signal that she should stop passing out information like that. But she mistook my action as a manifestation of endearment, smiled back sweetly at me and kept right on going.

"Actually, we were in Lissewege today, a beautiful little village. Do you know it?"

"Oh, yes, yes," Rolph offered. "It's a fine little town. But how did you know to go see Lissewege? Did somebody tell you about it, or did you just see it in one of the tour books?"

I reached under the table again, but this time I literally dug my fingers into her lithe knee and gave her a warning look. She looked back at me reproachfully with pain and concern in her eyes.

"We read about it in a tour book," she lied, trying to cover up her slip about us having business in the Bruges area. "At least I did. It has a very Flemish flavor, and when I think of Belgium, I always think of Flanders."

Rolph changed the subject. "Oh, well, what do you folks do for a living in the United States?" he asked.

Returning to her blabby mode, Rosanne pointed to me and said that I was a lawyer, and then went on to describe herself as, "of all things," an accountant. Rolph then declared that by looking at us, he would have thought it was vice versa, that I looked more the part of a numbers juggling accountant.

"What kind of lawyer are you, Winston?" he asked.

"An honest one," I jumped in, laughingly, before Rosanne could reveal anything else.

"I didn't know there were such lawyers," Rolph parried.

"Yes," I said, "there are. We're all very poor."

He laughed, straining to finish off our little repartée on this subject. "I very much doubt that you're all poor, Mr. Barchrist. If I had to guess what type of lawyer you were, I'd guess you were a criminal lawyer."

"No, I'm not, actually," I replied. "Why would you guess that?"

"Because there used to be this somewhat stocky lawyer on the television in the States called Perry Mason, and somehow you remind me of him a little."

"Well, I'm no Perry Mason," I insisted.

Oh, he's being modest," Rosanne chimed in. "Actually, he does do a little criminal work, criminal defense."

"Well, if I ever get to Columbus, Ohio, and I have need of your services, I'll remember that," Rolph said, giving me a fist bump on the shoulder and smiling, as if he never would have such a need. "Say, that reminds me. We had a young guy, well-known as an amateur weight lifter around here who went to Columbus, Ohio, for a competition and died there under very questionable circumstances. Some people say he was murdered. Have you ever heard of that situation?"

A lump suddenly caught in my throat. Was Bruge Biliuss that well known in this part of Belgium? Who really was this Rolph Van Heyde, that he actually knew about Biliuss' death? Of all the people sitting in the square this evening, how did he happen to pick us as people with whom to strike up a conversation? I decided to pursue the matter a little further with him.

"No," I said, "I haven't heard about any weight lifter who died in Columbus. What did he die of?"

"Nobody here seems to know," Van Heyde answered. "He was just found dead under what people are calling 'questionable circumstances.'"

"Well, was this matter carried in the local newspapers here?"

"Yes, I think so."

Suddenly, the bells in the Belfort began playing. They were playing Beethoven's *Fur Elise,* and when it ended, a low resonating bell struck the same note nine times.

"Well, 9:00 p.m.," Rolph said, as he rose from the table. "It's time for me to go. Where are you good folks staying here in Bruges?"

I heard Rosanne take a breath readying herself to say the name of our hotel, and I quickly kicked her under the table. Instead, she said, "Oh. I can never remember the name of the place, but I have it here somewhere in my purse," and she began fumbling and scrambling through her purse, waiting for me to say something that would save her bacon.

"No matter," Rolph said. "Here's my card. I've enjoyed talking with you, and if I can be of any help in the future during your stay in Bruges, please don't hesitate to contact me." Then he drained the remaining beer in his glass and walked away.

Rosanne and I looked down at his card:

Rolph T. K. Van Heyde
PHARMAE BRUXELLES LTD.
A Division of Aiden Life Corporation

CHAPTER TWENTY

By the morning, Rosanne had calmed down from me kicking her and chiding her under the table the night before, which she considered to be very rude, disrespectful and out of place. She took her nose out of the newspaper long enough to say, "From now on, if you want me not to say something, just say 'excuse me, I need to talk to you for a minute.' Then we can get up from wherever we are, leave for a minute, and go somewhere to discuss it. That way, I'll know what's going on instead of just feeling like an idiot."

"I'm sorry," I said. "It won't happen again. Now could you just put that paper down and talk to me?"

"Look at this!" she said, showing the *Walloon Gazietta*. It was printed in French. "It says Janic Vadea will be directing an outdoor symphony concert given by the *Flandereen*—that must mean their orchestra—here in Bruges tonight at the Burg. Can you imagine that? Janic Vadea, what's he doing here? Where is the Burg?"

"It's another town square, but smaller than where we were last night, near the police station, I think."

"Shall we go?"

"Yes, I don't see why not, if we can finish up our business today at Pharmae Bruxelles in time for it. I wonder how Vadea managed to get himself booked in Bruges."

. . .

Pharmae Bruxelles, Ltd. operated a moderately sized administrative and research complex from a modern green ceramic brick box building outside Bruges in a small city called Tourhout. An employee directory at the front desk and inadequate security made it easy to locate Niels Blenker, Hans van Kugee and Felix de Wolff, the three co-worker friends of Bruge Biliuss whose names Geertje had reluctantly given us. But actually speaking with them was quite a bit more difficult. All of them spoke English, but only one, Niels Blenker, agreed to meet with us off the site of the research building for lunch.

Blenker turned out to be a body builder also, and a fairly jealous one. He told us he felt the company should have sent him along with Biliuss to the Schwarzenegger event in Columbus. He claimed he had worked as hard as Bruge on the NSTC project for the cure of Parkinsons, the only difference being that while his job involved the testing of Ragasiline on animals, Bruge was charged with quantifying the drug's results on humans. Approximately 70 employees had worked on the research and development for the project. In addition to bonusing them all for their work, the company had chosen to hand out five special awards to those whom it considered to be the top researchers on the NSTC agenda. Niels was one of those people, but instead of an opportunity to go to the Schwarzenegger Classic in America, he was given a free membership to the most popular gym in Bruges for five years.

"Did you use the company's anabolic steroid product?"

"Oh, yes."

"Did Bruge?"

"Oh yes, we both did, as did all the other body builders who worked there."

"There were others?"

"Maybe five or six of us."

I looked at Niels as he was talking. He was bigger than Bruge, and more handsome and athletic looking. Furthermore, unlike Bruge, he had a full head of hair, and overall, he just looked stronger.

"I just don't understand what the company felt Bruge had that I didn't," he complained. "I mean, why the difference? I feel I had just as much of a chance of winning that competition as Bruge Biliuss, and I would have made just as good a representative for Pharmae Bruxelle, Ltd. as Bruge for product endorsement purposes."

"Who do you suppose might be able to answer the question why the company chose Bruge over you?" Rosanne asked.

"I don't know," Niels replied. "The person who knew the most about what he was actually doing for the company was Felix."

"Felix de Wolff?" Rosanne asked. "But he won't talk to us."

"He might," Niels replied. "Felix is just an extremely careful man. He knows the company doesn't want us talking to any outsiders about this project. But if you were to give me a phone number he could call, he might just call it. He's a very jittery man, and Bruge's death seems to have unnerved him a little. He just doesn't want to expose himself to anyone here in Tourhout, or in Bruges for that matter, as an employee who would talk to outsiders."

"Here, give him this number and tell him to call me at our hotel," I told Niels. "It's not a cell phone, so there should be no security problems, especially if he doesn't call from a land line traceable to him."

Our trip to Pharmae Bruxelles had turned out to be a bust. We didn't get any information from Niels Blenker, other than the fact that there were other weight lifters at the company. Our interview with Geertje hadn't yielded much more. Was something being held back from us? My instincts told me this was so, and my suspicion was soon confirmed.

About an hour after we arrived back at our hotel room, the room phone rang. It was a very circumspect and reluctant Felix de Wolff.

"I suppose you've talked to Geertje Biliuss about how her husband happened to wind up going to the United States," he said.

I gave no response.

"Did she give you Niels' name?" he asked. "Did she give you mine?"

I continued not to respond.

"How did Bruge die?" he asked.

"Murdered," I responded.

"Ach—the phone went silent for almost half a minute—that's what I thought."

"Mr. de Wolff, Niels seemed to think you might have some information as to why the company selected Bruge instead of him to go to Columbus for the Schwarzenegger Competition. Do you?"

"Information, no, I have only a theory. Let us just say that Bruge may have been selected on the basis of some information he had that Niels did not have."

"And what information was that?"

"I should have said, on the basis of information he *said* he had. I don't know if he actually had such information."

"And I ask you again, Mr. de Wolff, what information was that?"

"You'll have to get that from Geertje Biliuss."

"Well, do you know what the information is, Mr. de Wolff?"

There was a click as he hung up the phone. I sat down heavily on the bed, replacing the phone receiver into its carriage. Here I was in Bruges, having travelled all the way from the United States, only to have a conversation with Bruge Biliuss' wife, in which I found out next to nothing, and then a conversation with Niels Blenker which achieved the same result, and now this. *There's something important going on here, and the only reason I don't know what it is, is because people are refusing to tell me,* I thought to myself.

"Rosanne,"—she was in the bathroom—"we have to get the interpreter tomorrow and go out to see Geertje Biliuss in Lissewege again."

"Ok," she called back from the shower. "Do we have the time to eat and get to that Vadea concert tonight? I think we do."

"OK, we'll go," I said.

When we got to the Burg, we saw that a temporary band shell had been erected at one end of the square. People were walking all around it, and there were microphone testers working on the stage. Directly across from the band shell, there was a large portable bleacher stand filled with red plastic chairs. Townspeople were already beginning to occupy the chairs.

Slowly, the orchestra players began mounting the temporary stage; taking out their instruments and tuning them. Below the stage, Janic Vadea could be seen pacing back and forth, talking with a gaggle of people, probably municipal officials. Then he walked over to an alcove in the white brick police station, where another man joined him, and the two talked there alone.

"Well, would you look at that!" Rosanne said, pointing toward the police station. "Isn't that the man who was talking to us last night in the other square?"

"Rolph?"

"Yeah, Rolph. It looks like he and Vadea are talking to each other like they're old friends. I'm half tempted to go down there and say hello."

"Let's do it," I said.

So we went down to the police station door and acted like obnoxious tourists, waiting for a break in their conversation so we could jump in. Rolph looked confused when he saw us but quickly recovered. Vadea looked perplexed and disturbed.

"Do I know you?" Vadea asked tentatively, looking into my eyes and searching his memory.

"These are my friends from Columbus, Ohio, that I met last night, Janic," Rolph said. Then turning toward us, he said, "This is Janic Vadea. He used to work in your home town. You might even know of him. He used to be—"

"The director of the Columbus Symphony Orchestra," I said.

"—Right!" Rolph continued.

"Now I remember," Vadea piped up, focusing his dark eyes on me like lasers. "We met one day in the orchestra practice room. You were there with Igor Bashenko."

"Yes, that's correct," I replied, remembering that uncomfortable meeting where Bashenko took over from Vadea. "So tell me," I said, trying to change the subject. "How do the two of you know each other?"

"Oh, I guess you could say we have a mutual friend," Rolph said, flashing his gold eye tooth at me as he smiled. For the first time, I noticed that his straight, sandy red hair was combed over to one side of his head, reminiscent of Hitler's hair cut. Rolph did not volunteer the name of their mutual friend, and figuring it was none of my business, I did not ask it.

CHAPTER TWENTY ONE

It was 9:30 p.m. in Bruges and we had just gotten back from the Janic Vadea concert at the Burg. The time difference between Belgium and Columbus was six hours, making it 3:30 a.m. there, but I knew Trudy would still be up because she never goes to bed before 6:00 a.m. Trudy Fischel was a consummate night owl. So I called her. Why not? I had just experienced an insight, which was sort of like my own little epiphany!

Looking at Rolph Van Heyde, with his straight Hitler-like hair, standing next to Janic Vadea earlier that evening, had suddenly reminded me that Ronnie Herimus had described the stranger who had visited him in his kitchen on the day Bruge Biliuss was murdered as having sandy red hair combed over like Adolph Hitler's, just like Rolph's hair was combed. Ronnie had also remembered the first name of this man's company as Pharmacy or something like that, and Rolph's card said he worked for Pharmae Bruxelles, LTD. Could Rolph have been the stranger who had visited Ronnie on the morning of the murder? He said he'd never been to Columbus, but...

"Trudes, how much will it cost me to have you break into two computers? The first belongs to Pharmae Bruxelles, Ltd., of Tourhout, Belgium. The second is the Interpol computer in Lyon, France. I'm looking for information on a man named Rolph T. K. Van Heyde...everything you can find on him, including his travels to Columbus, Ohio, if any."

"Interpol! That's going to be pretty expensive counselor...let's say $5000."

"Trudes..."

"OK, $3000."

"Deal—I want to know every time he's travelled to Columbus, if ever, who paid his air fare, where he stayed in Columbus, where else he's visited, what his association is with Janic Vadea, the former conductor of the Columbus Symphony, and anything else you can get on him. I'll call back to see what you've found in a couple of days."

After hanging up on Trudy, I turned to Rosanne. "Tomorrow, I think you should interview Geertje Biliuss again without me. Maybe she'll feel more comfortable talking just woman to woman. You need to find out from her what information Bruge could have had that caused the company to select him to go to the Schwarzenegger Classic in Columbus instead of Niels Blenker."

"OK, I'd like to rent a bike and ride it out to Lissewege though. The ride along the canal is supposed to be beautiful, and, you know, this is supposed to be a vacation for me, as well as a working trip for you."

"Well, you'll need the interpreter there too, but I can bring her out in the car and drop her off at the Biliuss house when you get there."

"Sounds good to me."

The next morning, we awoke to an article in the *Walloon Gazietta,* which Rosanne liked to read every morning to test out her French. A small story in the second section announced that Niels Blenker, an employee of Pharmae Bruxelles, Ltd. had died mysteriously during the night. Foul play was suspected. The police were investigating.

"This is the same man we talked to just yesterday," Rosanne said. "It's very alarming."

"Yes, it makes me very uncomfortable too," I replied. "It's very strange."

We rode out along the canal to Lissewege, Rosanne on a rented bike, and with me following in the Renault *Merd* with the interpreter. As I dropped off the interpreter, I again noticed a man across the canal leaning against his parked bicycle. He was facing Geertje's house. When I came back an hour later to pick up the interpreter, he was still there.

A very excited Rosanne accompanied the interpreter out to the car and started to tell me what she had learned. As she was talking, I noticed the man across the canal was still watching us. So I told Rosanne that she should hold off and tell me all about it later. I wanted to get out of there and see if the man left when we left.

Rosanne mounted her bike and began to leave. I watched as the man also mounted his bike and began to follow her down the canal road back toward Bruges. The man, however, remained on the other side of the canal. I reached over into the glove box and pulled out a pair of opera glasses left there from the concert the night before, and I took a better look at him.

His straight, sandy red hair was combed over to one side like Hitler's. It was Rolph Van Heyde!

I followed Rosanne and Rolph down the canal, being particularly alert at every bridge to see if Rolph crossed over to Rosanne's side of the canal, but he didn't. As I was doing this, I began to interrogate the interpreter about what Geertje had said to Rosanne.

"She tell her she tink Pharmae Bruxelles selected Bruge Biliuss for da trip to da States because he knew someting nobody else knew."

"And what was that?"

"Dat de embryonic stem cell research was used in de product, Ragasaline, dat dey introduced on de market to cure Parkinson's disease. She tink dey give Bruge the big trip to da U.S.A wit promise of an endorsement contract so he would, how you say, 'keep his mouth closed.'"

When I heard this, I must have involuntarily speeded up. I don't know if it was because I wanted to talk to Rosanne some more about this, or because I was afraid for some reason that Rolph was following her because he wanted to hurt her. I don't think she knew she was being followed. When we got back to Bruges, I dropped the interpreter off and headed straight for our hotel. Rosanne had beaten me back to the room, and she must have gotten tired waiting for me because there was a note:

"Meet me for a coffee at the Market Square. I'll be at one of the tables on the right.   R"

I got to the square just in time to see her across the huge expanse and disappearing with Rolph into the Belfort. Her bike was locked to one of the tables with another note on it:

"Back in 20 minutes or so—our new found tour guide is showing me the bells in the tower.   R"

New found guide?—oh my God, she was going up in the tower with Rolph. I looked up at the Belfort with its carillon, open to the air 250 feet up, and suddenly an inexplicable fear for Rosanne's well-being gripped me. I sprinted across the square to the Belfort, not an easy task for somebody who weighs over 300 pounds. By the time I got into the tower, I was winded. Nonetheless, I began calling up to Rosanne to come down, as I forced myself to begin mounting the 366 stairs to the top. My heart was pounding in my chest ominously. Climbing those steps was too strenuous for a man in my shape. But I couldn't let her continue toward the top with Rolph. As far as I was concerned, the man's *bona fides* had been compromised by his following us back from Lissewege twice, by his strange relationship with Janic Vadea, by saying he'd never been to Columbus, by supposedly telling Ron Herimus that Bruge wasn't using the company's steroid product when other evidence pointed to the fact that he was. The facts surrounding Rolph were very complex. He could be dangerous. What if, for some reason, he tried to push Rosanne off the top of the tower?

"Rosanne, RosANNE, come down!" I yelled, my voice echoing but muffled in the close space of the circular stairwell.

I had managed to get almost half way up the structure and I was on the verge of collapsing, when suddenly I looked up, and there she was coming down the steps with Rolph behind her.

"My goodness, Winston, what are you doing?" she asked.

"Oh,"...and, I did collapse, panting and gasping for breath.

I couldn't speak. Rolph and Rosanne had to sit there until I came to, and then they had to steady me as we went slowly back down the stairs.

The last thing I remember was Rosanne saying, "Winston, you're so pale!"

CHAPTER TWENTY TWO

The next morning, I awakened to Rosanne's business voice. She was speaking into our room telephone to KLM, attempting to convince the airline that our reservations back to Columbus needed to be changed to today or tomorrow. She kept reiterating that there was an emergency.

"What emergency?" I asked.

She shushed me with her hand, pointing to the phone, trying to keep me from interrupting her conversation with the airline agent. Finally, when it was clear she was on hold, I repeated, "What emergency?"

"What emergency? Your health. That's what! You should have seen how you looked yesterday when Rolph and I brought you back here. He had to come up to the room with me to help me get you into bed."

"You showed him where we were staying...our hotel, our room, everything?"

"Yes, Winston. What's going on with you? Why are you acting so weird? That little gambit you pulled yesterday, running up the steps of the Belfort, shouting my name. What was that all about? You could have killed yourself!"

"Rolph is an evil man. I was afraid he was going to take you up into that tower and push you off."

"What?"

"Yes, I was trying to stop him from doing that, and I did."

"Winston, that's crazy... Rolph is a very nice man."

"Very nice men don't follow women back from Lissewege, but that's what he was doing to you."

"What? That's crazy, Winston."

"Is it? Well, I watched it with my own eyes. Also, very nice men don't show up at my friend Ronnie's house telling him that Bruge Biliuss is refusing to use the products of his own company, when Bruge is actually using them."

"I don't understand a thing you're saying. What are you talking about, Winston?"

"And nice men don't just materialize out of nowhere and befriend a woman who is helping me investigate a crime. He's dangerous, Rosanne. I tell you, he's dangerous!"

"Winston, Rolph Van Heyde is not dangerous, and I don't know what you're talking about, but even if you're right, and he's dangerous—all the more reason for us to get out of here now. That little incident with you trying to run up the steps may have taken its toll on your heart, and we need to check that out right away. We're going home—ASAP."

"But what about Ronnie's defense?"

"You can work on that from home. We're leaving."

"No."

"Yes!"

"Well, I won't go!"

. . .

Our plane landed at Kennedy International about 8:00 a.m. the next day. Three hours later, we would arrive in Columbus. Rosanne was busy trying to decide if she should take me to the doctor, or whether we should just go straight to the emergency room at the hospital. I was trying to decide if I should go to my office when we landed, or go directly to the police station first and start clearing things up for Igor. Except for these subjects, we weren't talking to each other. I felt fine. She kept trying to convince me I looked terrible. "It's merely jet lag," I groused, annoyed with her motherly pestering.

Once on the ground in Columbus, I went straight to my office. I called Trudy for a report on her computer break-in at Interpol and about what she'd found out about Rolph Van Heyde so far.

"The man travels extensively. He was in Columbus three times this year, the latest being at the beginning of this month. There were no credit card records revealing where he stayed. He also moves around Europe quite a bit: last year, five trips to Belgrade in Serbia, and various trips around Western Europe. He's a Sales Representative for a company called Pharmae Bruxelles, Ltd.—something to do with drugs. His compensation appears to be by straight commission. Oh, and get this! Interpol carries his name in their records on a wanted list for engaging in the production of embryonic stem cell lines in Germany, a prohibited practice in that country. How arcane is that? And, he's been arrested there for the illegal possession of a fire arm. Apparently Germany has very strict gun control laws."

"That helps me quite a bit, Trudes. The man *has* been to Columbus, even though he says he hasn't been here, and he carries a gun. As for the business about stem cells, I don't understand that at all."

I hung up wondering what my next move could, or should be. Then it hit me like a flash! Geertje told Rosanne she thought Bruge received his trip to the Schwarzenegger Classic from Pharmae Bruxelles because he secretly knew that embryonic stem cells were used in the product, Ragasaline, recently introduced on the market in this country to cure Parkinson's disease. Rolph worked for Pharmae Bruxelles, a subsidiary of Aiden Life Pharmaceuticals, which was now making money hand over fist from this new product. What effect would news that embryonic stem cells played a role in the product have on the market price of Aiden Life's stock on the NYEX with all the political fallout concerning stem cell research in the United States? What if Conservatives began a campaign against Ragasaline, claiming human embryos were being destroyed through abortions to save the lives of Parkinson's patients that were practically over anyway. Was this why the company was insisting on such secrecy from its employees about the new product?

I called Trudy back. "Do me one more favor Trudes."

"These aren't favors. I don't do favors."

"OK then—here's one more job for you. A man in Tourhout, Belgium, named Niels Blenker recently died under questionable circumstances. Murder is suspected and there's going to be an autopsy. Please find out the specific cause of death from the autopsy report."

"That'll cost you $500."

"$250," I responded.

"No, I don't read Belgian—$500."

"OK, use your language programs. There's no such language called Belgian. The report will be either in Dutch or French."

"What...are you working for the King of Belgium now or something? Why all the interest in a Belgian murder?"

"Well, it might just have an impact on Ronnie Herimus' case in this country. That's why."

My office phone rang as soon as I hung up on Trudy. It was Igor Bashenko.

"Winston, you're back, thank God! I was calling to make an appointment through your secretary. As I said when we last talked, I need your help, and I need it fast.

"Mr. Dzugash is claiming that I kidnapped his wife, and he's pressing charges. Anastasia is upset and she has insisted I call you immediately."

"That's ridiculous," I replied. "I was there and I heard Ida agree to come to Columbus with you of her own free will. Maybe you should be pressing charges against him as a suspect who fired bullets at you during the first concert of the season. What have the police done to investigate that?"

"They got a warrant to do a ballistics tests with his guns and the bullets they found at the Ohio Theater. They didn't match."

"OK," I said, "so maybe my idea to press charges against Dzugash for shooting at you isn't such a good one. Tomorrow I'll go down to the CDP and tell them what I know about how Ida Dzugash got to Columbus. At least that should put an end to Dzugash's kidnapping charges. And by the way, Igor, maybe, just maybe, this whole little adventure with Ida should be a lesson to you to curb your obsessions with women in the future."

"I don't know, Winston. Something just comes over me that says I can have a certain woman I see if I want her, and bang—I go for it. I know I need to stop, but I don't know how to stop myself. You know when this happens, I love them all—and they love me. It's never just the sex. It's a real question I ought to be asking myself."

"Well, I may have an answer for you on that one. His name is Arnold Goldstein. Next time I Skype with him, I want you to be present so I can introduce you. We can't have the maestro of the Columbus Symphony Orchestra carrying on like this. Maybe you need Prozac or something."

CHAPTER TWENTY THREE

My trip to the police station on behalf of Igor Bashenko was very disconcerting, to say the least. Despite telling them Ida Dzugash came to Columbus voluntarily, they decided to charge Bashenko with kidnapping. Since I was already there, I also asked how Ron Herimus' case was proceeding; the answer to that was also disconcerting. Officer Shapiro told me Ron was being brought before the grand jury, not on manslaughter charges, but on murder two charges within the month. Anthony Picard shared with me on the "q-t" that Heinrich Wabstmann had brought a lot of pressure to bear in both situations: in Bashenko's case, on the police, and in Herimus' situation on the Prosecutor's Office. If somebody had accused Bashenko of kidnapping, Wabstmann definitely wanted him charged so the symphony organization could get to the bottom of it. If the evidence pointed to Herimus as Biliuss' killer, he wanted him indicted. As the richest man in Columbus, Wabstmann apparently had a lot of pull.

"In *both* situations!" I exclaimed. "I can understand why he might want Bashenko charged. He hates him. But what could his interest possibly in Ronnie's case?"

"I don't know, maybe the public interest," Picard opined. "All I know is that he's accused the prosecutor's office and the police of foot dragging and nobody wants to get on the dark side of that man. He's very influential."

"But why should Wabstmann care about Ron Herimus? He's just a simple guy who lives his life quietly below the radar."

"Heinrich Wabstmann is a very public personality in this town, and he's very interested in seeing to it that public institutions and events here reflect positively on the city. The murder at the Schwarzenegger Classic besmirches the reputation of an event for which the town is known in the eyes of people who aren't from Columbus. It will have the same effect that the death of a hockey fan at a Columbus Blue Jackets game a while back had, where a woman got hit in the head with a hockey puck. People think of that when they think of Columbus' hockey team, not that Columbus is a professional sports city. Wabstmann considers this town to be his personal fiefdom, and he has an interest in righting every public nick and scrape that mars its image."

"Yeah," added Shapiro, "the murder at the Schwarzenegger Classic has been an ongoing story for weeks in the national news, and now stories of Bashenko's elicit love dalliance are creeping into the *Dispatch* on a local level. Wabstmann hates all the bad publicity the city is getting."

It was true. A day or so later, Igor Bashenko informed me that the executive committee of the Columbus Symphony, which Wabstmann chairs, had placed him on administrative leave, pending the outcome of Dzugash's kidnapping allegations against him, and that they had gone so far as to invite Janic Vadea back to town from Serbia to finish the season. But what this really meant was Igor was finished at the Columbus Symphony Orchestra for good.

There was no way he could come out a winner. Even if he escaped criminal kidnapping charges by proving in a criminal trial that Ida came to Columbus with him voluntarily, which he could do, he would still be guilty of stealing another man's wife in the public's eye. And, it would probably be longer than a year before his case even came to trial. It also meant the Columbus Symphony itself was finished. The orchestra players were in utter rebellion over the executive board's decision to replace Igor with Vadea when they heard about it, but they were unable to show their disapproval by striking again because of the no-strike clause in their new contract. Igor feared that instead, they would resort to sabotage by messing up Vadea's offerings to the public during concerts at every turn.

"Where the score calls for fortissimo, they will play piano. Where it calls for largo, they will play stretto," he said. "Thus, *Beethoven's 5th* will have the force of Haydn's *45th Symphony*, and Dvorak's *Symphony No. 9* will sound like Mahler's *Symphony No. 9*. It will be terrible, after all the work we've done so far to rebuild. You know I've heard their favorite trick before the strike was to wait a second after the final crash in the finale of some huge piece, and then have a percussion player accidentally drop a triangle or a cymbal on the floor and completely ruin the mood. It infuriated Vadea."

"All your work will have been for nothing if that happens, Igor," I told him. "The symphony will lose its following and become known as a third rate city orchestra, even with Janic Vadea as its director."

"Wabstmann doesn't care. He has wanted me out of the way from the very beginning, and now he's gotten me out of the way," Bashenko whined. "I have a five year contract with the orchestra, but it says I can be terminated at any time for 'moral turpitude.' What does that mean?"

"I don't know, Igor, but something tells me we're going to find out. Have you ever heard of a legal claim for tortuous interference with a contract?"

"No."

"Well, that's what may be happening to you here. It's when someone tells a lie about someone, or does something else, that causes a third-party to break a contract with the party of the first part, or causes the party of the first-part to be unable to perform the contract."

"Wha...I don't understand the legal mumbo-jumbo," Igor protested. "Party of the first-part, third-party...who's the second party? Is there a party of the second-part...and anyway, in my case, who are these parties?"

"I'm not quite sure yet, but in your case I think they may be Heinrich Wabstmann, Janic Vadea, Joseph Dzugash, or Ida Dzugash, or maybe all of them together trying to get your contract broken," I replied. "We'd know for sure after a little discovery, maybe one or two depositions. It would be a civil case, not a criminal case, so we'd have discovery."

"Well, would you take a case like that, as an attorney, Winston?"

"Sure, for a one third contingency fee, with the client paying all the expenses up front. Why not? I mean I'd want to do a little more investigation into it first, and also I'd want to put a little more thought into it, and maybe some research—but yes."

"I mean, do you think I could win?"

"You didn't kidnap Ida Dzugash did you? What's Heinrich Wabstmann doing interfering with a police investigation of Joseph Dzugash's criminal charge against you? We know Ida lied about being kidnapped, don't we? And why does Janic Vadea seem to show up every time Heinrich Wabstmann wants to get rid of you? Yep, I think if we throw up enough of this stuff against the wall, some of it'll stick. Somebody is trying to interfere with your contract as conductor of the Columbus Symphony. The problem we're going to have is proving that it was done for malicious reasons, but what have you to lose?"

"What do you mean we'll have trouble proving it was done for malicious reasons? Don't you remember, Winston—somebody took a few pot shots at me on the opening night of the season, with real bullets."

"Yeah, but we don't know who that was, and I'm afraid we're going to have to let the police find out the answer to that one for us."

"So you're saying that if we can't prove malice, we'll lose, right?"

"Yeah, I think that's our downside," I answered. "Listen, Igor, why don't you think this whole thing over for a few days and get back to me. We don't have to be in a rush to file a suit against anybody."

In the mean time, I felt I should spend a little time with Ronnie telling him what I'd learned in Belgium. I took a package of the anabolic steroid manufactured by Pharmae Bruxelles with me over to his place and asked him if it was the drug the man who had visited him was trying to sell to him on the day Bruge Biliuss was murdered. He couldn't remember, but he said he thought it had more English on the package than the steroid I was holding.

"OK, tell me this, Ron. Are you sure this man said that Bruge Biliuss was refusing to take the drug the man had with him when he was in your house?"

"Yes, boss. I'm sure of that."

"Positive?"

"Yes, boss. Geez. Why do you keep asking me?"

"Because when I was in Flanders, I learned that Bruge Biliuss worked for a company with the first name of Pharmae, and he WAS taking that company's anabolic steroid. You thought the first name of the company this stranger who visited you worked for was Pharmacy, right?"

"Right—or something like that."

"OK, now, one more time, describe him for me."

"He was tall, with big hands, long arms, and sandy red hair."

"What did his face look like?"

"A box with his hair combed over to one side of it—very weird!"

"And his teeth?"

"Oh. Yeah, yeah...he had a prominent gold filling right here." Ron pointed to his upper left eye tooth. "I forgot to tell you that before."

CHAPTER TWENTY FOUR

Picup was insisting that Igor leave his house immediately. Anastasia was wailing tearfully, as the accomplished maestro sheepishly looked up at his daughter. On the table lay a summons headed, "State of Ohio vs. Igor Bashenko," summoning him to court for a preliminary pre-trial hearing on kidnapping charges. Anastasia had asked me to come over to explain how this all occurred, but now, instead, I was standing in their living room trying to bring order out of chaos.

"You have brought nothing but misery to your daughter for years," Picup was shouting at Igor, "always yelling and angry when it suited you, leaving her in Russia to come to the United States, because it suited your needs, not hers, cheating on her mother, withdrawing for weeks on end from everybody, acting like you have greater talents than you do, going on big overly expensive spending sprees, and now this! You bring dishonor to your family. I used to think you were just sick with your illicit romances and your foolish obsessions all the time, but no. You are a criminal. You manipulate to get what you want, and this time you got caught. And now, look at you. Now you're coming in here with your silly thoughts about suing somebody else for all this." Picup was yelling at the top of his lungs.

Earlier, I had asked Arnold Goldstein, during one of our sessions, what manic depressive people were like. I wondered if they were bad people, or hopelessly mentally ill. I was wondering if we could use the insanity defense to get Igor off from the kidnapping charges.

"Bi-polar people are like your friend Igor Bashenko," he said, "often very good, very artistic and imaginative, sometimes very kind, very human people, who can bring a lot of joy to others, but sometimes too much joy, while not realizing the ill effects they have on the people around them. But insane, Winston, what's the definition of insanity? Who isn't insane? No, manic depression is just a disease like diabetes or something, and, except in the most rampant cases, it can be treated. Was John Kennedy insane? Were Winston Churchill or Abraham Lincoln? What about Julius Caesar? Many people think they were all manic depressives. Indeed, many people think it was their diseases that allowed them to become great when they needed to be."

"Thanks, Dr. Goldstein. I guess the insanity defense won't work then."

"Correct, Winston; that'll be $60.00. We ran over a little today."

The question facing me now, as I stood in the Andropov living room, was not how to defend Igor, but how to extract myself from the dysfunctional family scene that was unfolding before me. While Picup raged on, Anastasia was becoming more and more morose, and Igor was withdrawing into a cloud of depression. The look on his face must have been just like the look on George Washington's face after he got caught chopping down the cherry tree...shame.

I decided that the answer was to remove Picup from the scene temporarily, so I asked him to come outside with me to discuss renting the limo for use in one of my other cases. I had no use for the limousine, and it was just a ruse to get him out of the house for a little while so things could cool down.

Picup was seething. He reached under the front seat of the limo as he spoke, bending down and exerting himself as if he was feeling around for something. "He ruins my wife's life with his crazy antics, and he is ruining our marriage."

Out came a .357 Magnum from under the seat, just like the one Joseph Dzygash had been flashing around the Andropov house a few weeks back.

"I keep this in the car for defensive purposes," Picup commented aimlessly, pointing the barrel of the gun toward the sky and smiling at it approvingly. He smirked. "Sometimes I think, what would happen if I used it on my beloved father-in-law?"

"Picup, you wouldn't—"

"Wouldn't what?" he dared.

"—Intentionally hurt anybody with that."

"Oh, of course not, Winston, but don't forget. I am a Russian, an angry, hot blooded Russian." Then he broke into a forced laugh, adopting a fake ominous look.

I had always thought of Picup as a simple man, docile and compliant, who shrank back in the presence of his much more educated and demonstrative wife, a vodka drinker and a checkers player, not smart enough for chess. This was a new Picup I was seeing, one with all of those qualities, but one who was also dangerously and carelessly wielding a large gun.

"Why are you holding that gun, Picup?"

"Oh, I don't know," he answered. "Sometimes I check to make sure it's still here. Anastasia doesn't like it very much, so I have to check when she's not around."

"You know," I said, "I did not realize the depth of your ill feelings toward your father-in-law, Picup."

"I have hated him for a long time. He gave us the money to buy this limousine and start the business, but he never misses an opportunity to remind us of that, and he has Ani—how you say—twirled around his little finger. When he calls, she comes."

"Twisted."

"What?"

"Twisted, not twirled."

"Whatever—anyway, as you can see, who could live with this? And now he brings disgrace on us."

"There's no disgrace unless he's convicted of the charge against him."

"Oh, but he's lost his job, hasn't he? And a very public job it is. Not only that, but we're stuck with him living here in the same city as us—on top of us, if you will."

Picup was right. Igor hadn't been convicted of anything. Yet he'd lost his job, and clearly Heinrich Wabstmann was behind it all. Why? What possible interest could Wabstmann have in getting Igor out of the symphony conductor's position that could justify going to the extent of getting him charged with a crime in what was nothing but a domestic fight between Ida and Joseph Dzygash? I figured the best place to start looking for the answer to that question was Art Malone. But that would have to wait until I could calm Picup down.

"Picup, put that gun away safely and don't take it out again unless someone attacks you while you're driving the limousine. Like you said, the gun is for self-defense. It's not for anything else. Let's go back in the house, and I will get your father-in-law out of there so you can leave him alone and he can leave you alone. Then I'm going to see what I can do about getting the maestro his job back."

After convincing Igor to leave the house, I went back to my office and put a call through to Malone. "What's Heinrich Wabstmann's interest in getting rid of Igor Bashenko?" I asked. "Who's he going to get to take his place?"

"He's already seen to the answer to your second question," Art offered. "He's bringing Vadea back to finish the season."

"Well, what's his obsession with Janic Vadea? This is the second time he's tried to give Bashenko's job back to Vadea. What is there between the two of those men?"

"That may be the answer to your first question, Winston. Vadea may be the reason Wabstmann's so interested in getting rid of Bashenko. That way, he can get Vadea back here. I think there is something more between the two of them than just the music connection. Vadea's family happens to be into pharmaceutical research in the Balkan area of Europe in a big way. Not too many people know that, but before the former Yugoslavia broke up, the Vadeas ran a huge research lab there."

"What did they research?"

"They were into the area of embryonic stem cell research. Stem cells and stem cell chains were easy to come by in the Balkans...no laws against abortion and no regulations prohibiting the research like in the more religious countries of Europe. Hell, Yugoslavia was a communist nation."

"But what's that got to do with Janic Vadea?" I asked. "He's a musician, not a biology researcher."

"Yes, but he's also the head of the Vadea family in Serbia, which is a very old aristocratic family. To do any business with the family, first Janic Vadea has to be kept happy."

"How do you know all this, Art?"

"Let's just say I've made it my hobby to keep up on what Heinrich Wabstmann, does, who he associates with, and why. Maybe it's because Wabstmann's always been so kind to me—laugh out loud."

"Are you sure of this information, Art?"

"My friend, you can take it to the bank. You can walk into any casino in Vegas and bet on it. There's nothing that little Gerry does that isn't for the sake of business, for the sake of making money. I know that for a fact, and if he has to keep Janic Vadea happy in order to get something from his family, he'll do whatever it takes...including finding him an orchestra to direct so he can advance his music career."

"Do you think there's any way to convince Wabstmann to back off his decision to fire Bashenko?" I asked.

"Not without leverage and lots of it."

"Well, isn't the Wabsmann/Vadea connection leverage of a sort?"

"You would have to be able to prove it. How are you going to do that?"

"Have you ever heard of something called a suit for the malicious interference with contract, Art?"

"No, but it sounds like fun."

"Well, if you want, I'll explain it to you, because I think Igor Bashenko may have a claim for malicious interference with contract against Heinrich Wabstmann, if what you say is true."

"Try me, Winston; I might like it."

"OK, and if you do like it, maybe the two of us should go talk to Wabstmann about it together. I know he's not going to listen to anything I have to say on my own."

CHAPTER TWENTY FIVE

Igor Bashenko vs. Heinrich Wabstmann, et al. was filed in the Court of Common Pleas of Franklin County two weeks after I explained the tort of malicious interference with contract to Art Malone. Excited about the prospects the suit had for exposing Wabstmann, Malone agreed to pay all expenses associated with the case. He then talked Igor Bashenko into becoming the plaintiff. Janic Vadea, and Joseph and Ida Dzygash were joined as parties-defendant. My fee for services was strictly contingent. Picup Andropov was beside himself, vowing Igor would suffer greatly for embarrassing the family by bringing the suit.

The first deposition to be taken in the suit was that of Janic Vadea who had just returned to the United States. I was at my best as a cross examiner, if I say so myself. I had to be. Art Malone was sitting at my side. I plunged headlong into a "fishing expedition."

Q. Tell me about the embryonic stem cell research that has been conducted by your family's research laboratory?

OPPOSING ATTORNEY: Objection! That's not relevant.

Q. We think it is. Shall we call on the Court to have him compelled to answer?

OPPOSING ATTORNEY. Go ahead and answer.

A. We have more embryonic stem cell lines than any other company in Europe or the Western Hemisphere.

Q. And why is that?

A. Because the laws in Eastern Europe permit this, whereas those of the Western European countries don't.

Q. Is that because there is no regulation on abortion in the Balkans?

A. I don't know.

Q. And has your family's company made these stem cell lines available to the Aiden Life Company, Heinrich Wabstmann's enterprise?

OPPPOSING ATTORNEY: Objection! You don't have to answer that. Don't answer. Let them go to Court and get an order ordering you to answer if they can.

Q. Tell me, Mr. Vadea, who controls your family's research organization?

A. As the head of the family, I guess I do.

Q. And, what is your relationship with Heinrich Wabstmann all about?

A. He's the head of the Columbus Symphony board of trustees, and I have been an employee of that board in the past, and I am presently, I guess, as the director of the orchestra.

Q. Is that your only association with him?

A. I don't know what you mean.

Q. Are you friends?

Suddenly Vadea's eyes fixed on mine like the defensive computerized trackers of a fighter jet in a skirmish with an enemy plane. He became alert and ready for combat.

A. He has been to my estate in Belgrade, where we have ridden horses together and played chess, yes, if you can call that friendship.

Q. You have an estate?

A. My family is a very old one.

Q. Tell me have you ever entertained Heinrich Wabstmann at your estate in Serbia for other than reasons of friendship? For instance, reasons having to do with your position as head of your family's research organization?

A. He has visited in his capacity as chairman of the Columbus Symphony.

Q. That's not what I was asking?

I could see that if this irate Serb could have fired the 20 millimeter wing cannons of the hypothetical war jet he was flying at me, he'd be pressing the trigger right now. Instead, he leaned over to confer with his lawyer. Their conference took longer than five minutes, but finally Vadea looked up.

A. No, he answered.

Q. No, what?

A. No, to your last question.

Games—we're starting to play games, I thought to myself. *I need to keep forging ahead. If Vadea doesn't want to talk about his family's business dealings for whatever reason, let's move on for now. Try another tack.*

Q. Mr. Vadea, let's move on. You know a man named Rolph T. K Van Heyde, don't you?

A. Yes, I do.

He seemed to be really squirming now, nervous and uncomfortable in his skin.

Q. What is your relationship with him?

A. He's a friend.

Q. What is his relationship with Heinrich Wabstmann?

A. Friends. They are friends.

Q. And how do you know this?

A. The three of us have been together at various times.

Q. And where was that? Here in *Columbus* or in Europe?

A. Both.

Q. And what brought the three of you together?

A. I don't remember—music probably.

It looked like that was as far as I was going to get for today, I thought to myself. *We had established, shockingly, that these three people knew each other and had been together. Why, I still didn't know? Obviously, Van Heyde had lied to me in Bruges. He'd been to the United State before, just as Trudy had reported. How this could have been the makings of a conspiracy to cause a breach of Igor Bashenko's contract with the Columbus Symphony Orchestra I had no idea. But one thing was for certain. Heinrich Wabstmann had been in contact with both men, and it wasn't just over the Columbus Symphony. Something inside me said now was not a good time to press the issue of why they had been together. Besides, Vadea was looking at his watch and fidgeting in his chair now. He realized my questions were approaching sensitive ground, and he probably was in no mood to answer truthfully. He was getting ready to lie. In other words, I needed more background information as a prelude to getting him to tell the truth.*

Q. Just a couple more questions Mr. Vadea. Do you know anyone named Joseph Dzygash?

A. No.

Q. Do you know a woman named Ida Dzygash?

A. No.

Q. Ever heard of either of them?

A. No.

I wasn't sure how far I'd gotten, but I knew I'd made headway. I didn't really believe all of Vadea's testimony was truthful, but one thing was established for sure. Heinrich Wabstmann and Rolph Van Heyde were linked. Whether the Dzygashs were a part of any conspiracy to interfere with Igor's contract with the symphony was a question that would have to wait until later in the discovery process. As for now, all I wanted to do was return to my desk and consider everything.

CHAPTER TWENTY SIX

A phone message from Trudy was waiting for me when I returned to the office. It was written in the perfect cursive Marinda was so proud of, almost like the German handwriting of the middle ages.

The note read, "Broken hyoid bone, Niels Blenker died of broken hyoid, according to autopsy report from Tourhout, Belgium. Bone crushed with no marks on the subject's neck. Please send $250 by week's end.— Trudy Fischel."

That's what Bruge Biliuss' autopsy indicated he had died of—a broken hyoid! Was it more than just coincidence that Biliuss and Blenker had died of the same cause? I was beginning to get a headache trying to keep Igor's case separate from Ronnie's in my mind. Niels Blenker dies of a broken hyoid, just like Bruge Biliuss. Both men were Belgian, as is Rolph Van Heyde, but Rolph may have been the man who showed up in Ronnie Herimus' kitchen in Columbus on the day Bruge Biliuss died. Rolph Van Heyde and Janic Vadea were friends, and, strangely, both men had a friend in common—Heinrich Wabstmann. Heinrich Wabstmann seemed to want to get rid of Igor Bashenko and to put Janic Vadea back into his position. Why? Rolph Van Heyde had been clearly following us around in Belgium. Why?

What did I know about the backgrounds of each of these men? Van Hyde was a liar. That was for sure. He also worked for a subsidiary of Wabstmann's company. Vadea was a musical aristocrat who headed up a family business steeped in pharmacological research. Although his true home was in Belgrade, Serbia, a relationship between him and Heinrich Wabstmann was being carried on here in the United States, presumably because of Vadea's symphony work, that Wabstmann refused to discontinue long after it should have been ended when the Columbus Symphony strike was settled on the basis of Vadea's being let go as music director.

According to Art Malone, Wabstmann was an extremely conservative man, and a user of people who would stop at nothing to enrich himself, and to grab power. For what could he possibly be using both Rolph Van Heyde and Janic Vadea? And in any event, what did it all have to do with Igor Bashenko, except that Bashenko seemed to be in the way of Janic Vadea's becoming re-employed by the symphony?

Who hated Bashenko enough to attempt to kill him? None of these people actually hated Igor, with the possible exception of Janic Vadea. But who hated him enough to fire bullets at him? Ida Dzygash—maybe? Joseph Dzygash—maybe?

Now I realized I should have followed up on my line of deposition questions to Vadea. I should have asked him what sorts of things brought Wabstmann, Van Heyde and him together inside and outside the United States. I realized I had a good feeling for what type of person Rolph Van Heyde was, and a fairly good idea as to what Janic Vadea was, but I didn't know much at all about how Heinrich Wabstmann conducted himself.

The stilted stress of the deposition room was not the right place to find that out. I had to meet him outside the legal strictures of a deposition to really understand want he was like, and there was only one way to do that—through Art Malone. So I had Art set up a dinner for the three of us at the old Lindenhoff Restaurant (now called Lindy's) ostensibly to discuss a future settlement of Bashenko's lawsuit against Wabstmann.

Located on the corner of Mohawk and Beck Streets in German Village, and noted for its fine German cuisine and wines, Lindy's was an ideal venue for a meeting with Wabstmann. Fronted with a posh brass bar, divided off with a mahogany banister from a clattery front dining room with walnut wooden floors and expensive paintings on the walls, this charming restaurant contained a much quieter area up its carpeted stairs on the second floor. There, a large bar with private rooms just off the bar, looked out on an expansive screened veranda. Art and I got a table in one of the private rooms, of course, and seated ourselves to wait for Wabstmann, who apparently saw to it that he was always the last person to enter any meeting.

"It's going to be interesting to see who comes with him," Art commented. "Heinrich Wabstmann never goes anywhere in public without body guards. I wonder where he's going to park them in this place."

We then began discussing the tack we were going to take. Of course, we had no intention of reaching a settlement in the lawsuit. We just wanted to bring Wabstmann out, maybe see what he was like when he got angry. Art had already confirmed that Wabstmann was paranoid by telling me he used body guards.

"He's also very aggressive," Art added, "a man who'll stop at nothing to get what he wants."

But I also wondered whether the man was outgoing or reticent, whether he was opinionated or relaxed, whether he was smart, whether he was a phony. The door to our little private dining room suddenly opened and Heinrich Wabstmann entered. There was a very healthy-looking blond on his arm, who seemed to be about 45 years old. Art and I stood.

"Hello, I'm Heinrich Wabstmann," Wabstmann announced to me, "and this is Fraulein Liebshutz. I believe you've met Ms. Liebshutz before," he added, turning to Art and shaking his hand. He did not shake mine. It was startling for a moment to see Wabstmann, a man clearly in his sixties, with a younger woman like this, furling her bare arm around his, as if they were lovers. This was an aspect of Wabstmann I had not anticipated.

"Is Fraulein Liebshutz your lawyer?" I asked, looking at the woman. It was hard not to stare at her. She was very Nordic in appearance, giving off an aura of good health and strength with her relatively long golden locks, well developed arms, long legs, and powerful bare shoulders, reminiscent of an Olympic swimmer. She was wearing a low neckline and a silk dress with a slit up the thigh. Her eyes were a piercing blue; her manner was extremely assured; and she was loaded down with jewelry.

"No, Fraulein Liebshutz is my associate," Wabstmann replied, fobbing off the question without a real answer.

"Yes, I've seen the two of you together before," Art said, smirking.

"Well, Mr. Wabstmann, I'd like to begin by—"

"Let us begin by your telling me how it is that you happen to have a lawyer-client relationship with Mr. Bashenko," Wabstmann interrupted.

"—asking you if Mr. Vadea has been rehired permanently yet," I continued.

There was a hiatus of silence, and then I said, "Maybe we could begin with an exchange of information by you telling me about your relationship with Mr. Vadea, and me telling you about my relationship with Mr. Bashenko."

Wabstmann exhibited annoyance. His blond "associate" just sat there quietly. "Are you here to take my deposition without any court authority behind you?" he asked. "I'm certain you already know Janic Vadea and I are good friends, but what you really want to know is if there's any business relationship between us. Am I not right? Well, not to say there is or isn't any such relationship between us, let me tell you that I simply don't discuss my business with anyone outside of my organization." He looked at Fraulein Liebshutz and she smiled coldly.

Attempting to break the quickly thickening ice, I adopted another tack. "I know your business is indeed far-flung, Mr. Wabstmann. Recently, when I was in Belgium, I met someone who works for one of your subsidiaries there. He spoke very highly of you."

"And who might that have been?"

"Rolph T. K Van Heyde. He said he knew you."

"Funny, I can't seem to place him," the little ex-Hitler Youth Nazi lied—right to my face. "But then, again, I have thousands of people working for me," he said.

I decided not to pursue it. The fact that the man lied was information enough for me. Obviously, he hadn't read Vadea's deposition transcript carefully enough—another tell-tale aspect of this little Heine. Either he was in a big hurry, not a detail man, or he had relied on an incompetent person to summarize Vadea's deposition for him.

"I thought we were here to discuss a settlement of your meritless little lawsuit against me," Wabstmann continued. "Let me just say your allegation that I sought 'maliciously,' as you put it, to cause a rupture in Mr. Bashenko's contract with the Columbus Symphony Board is farcical—absolutely farcical."

"The suit doesn't say you broke the contract. It says you conspired with others to get it broken."

"Maliciously!"

"Yes, maliciously."

"That's absurd! With whom did I conspire?"

"The suit says you conspired with Janic Vadea, and once you found out Ida Dzugash had left her husband for my client, you indirectly conspired with Joseph Dzugash, whom you learned had raised kidnapping allegations with the police. Isn't that why you intervened at the police station?"

"Well, now, there's a spin on the facts that would make any newspaper reporter dizzy, wouldn't it?" Wabstmann snarled, turning to Fraulein Liebshutz and laughing heartily, whereupon she joined in. But her blue eyes glared at me and her jaw was so clenched the muscles in it were almost as defined as those in her arms.

"That's why we're here, Mr. Wabstmann," I continued, "to end this thing before the newspapers get a hold of it."

"I'm not afraid of the newspapers," Wabstmann barked. "I'd just tell them the truth. I told the police to get to the bottom of the matter quickly because the reputation of the Columbus Symphony was at stake. I am the president of the symphony board, you know."

"And what will you say to the national press?" I asked, "when they learn that at the same time you demanded that Ronald Herimus be indicted for the murder of Bruge Biliuss?"

"What? Bruge Biliuss? I don't know what you're talking about. Isn't that the story that's been in the papers about a weight lifter or someone like that? I don't know where you're getting your information. What are you talking about?" Wabstmann was clearly becoming irate now, so irate that Fraulein Liebshutz put her heavily ringed hand on his to get his attention, and leaned over to whisper something in his ear.

Then, recovering his "in-charge" demeanor, Wabstmann announced, "My associate here points out that it's obvious you have no real interest in settling this lawsuit, and she is suggesting that we leave."

"But we haven't had dinner yet, Heinrich," Art complained. "Their sauerbraten here is delicious. Why not stay?"

"Maybe another time, Art," Wabstmann replied, and he pulled back his chair from the table and exited with Ms. Liebshutz in tow.

"It's a real pleasure watching her leave a room from behind, isn't it?" Art opined, turning to me once they had gone. "You know, she's one of his body guards, don't you? She could probably snap your neck with one swift roundhouse kick if she wanted to."

I was in awe, but didn't want to let Art know it, so I told him I wasn't surprised.

"Well, where do we go on this merry-go-round next?" he asked.

"Damned if I know, Art," I said. "I think I'm going to have to take the next couple of days to think about that."

Except for the blond "muscle" he was walking around with, Wabstmann was everything I had imagined him to be: tough, arrogant, smart, impatient, controlling, etc. As Art had said, Wabstmann was a nut that could only be cracked with leverage and lots of it.

CHAPTER TWENTY SEVEN

A week later, I was standing on the curb at State and Third downtown, when Picup, who was on a job, wheeled his limo over just to say hello for a minute.

"Hey, Picup, what's up?"

"I'm on a job for Heinrich Wabstmann," he replied proudly, "driving around one of his foreign visitors. Heinrich's our biggest client."

"I didn't know that. How often does he hire you?"

"At least once a month—I've got to go. His guest's probably waiting for me at the door of the hotel right now."

I watched Picup pull the limo into the covered auto reception area of the Sheraton, just to my right. This establishment used to be the Hyatt Downtown Hotel. I also saw him get out of the car and open the back door for his client. I had to wipe my eyes to make certain they weren't deceiving me!

Was that...? Yes, yes, it was!.. I was watching Rolph Van Heyde getting into the car. What possessed me to take out my cell phone and snap a picture of Rolph and Picup, I don't know, but I did it. Then I called Rosanne.

"You're not going to believe this," I told her, "but I just watched Rolph Van Heyde get into Picup Andropov's limousine at the Sheraton Hotel downtown."

"Rolph? You mean he's here from Belgium? Whatever for do you suppose?"

"I don't know, but one thing's for sure. I'm going to find out."

"What are you going to do?"

"Follow them if I can get a cab. There are cabbies lined up right around the corner here on State Street waiting for fares at the hotel. I'll grab one of those."

"Be careful, Winston."

My cab ride turned out to cost $255 round trip, plus tip, a credit card charge that would stick in my budget's craw for over two months. Picup drove north on I-71 all the way out to the northern border of Columbus. Then he turned east onto the I-270 beltway around the city, until he reached the suburb of Westerville, where he exited the expressway. My driver followed him through downtown Westerville and into the countryside to the north, toward the Hoover Reservoir. The cabbie was very excited. I told him to "follow that car," like in the movies. As the meter ticked upwards, he told me I was the most interesting fare he'd had in ten years, small recompense for what this ploy was costing me. The road we followed clung to the eastern shore of Hoover Reservoir, working its way through a series of hairpin turns toward the little town of Galena in Delaware County.

Hoover Reservoir is one of three impoundments supplying the City of Columbus with its water. To get to the east side of this man-made lake, one has to cross an impressive structure called Hoover Dam. It's no mere levee or dike built of dirt, but rather a 2583 foot long cement structure, wide enough for a two-lane road across its top. It rises 94 feet above the stream it intercepts, and it has a 680 foot wide spillway.

Delaware County, Ohio, at the north end of Hoover Reservoir, used to be a sleepy place with rolling hills, woods and streams, dedicated to farming and small town living, and known principally for the Ohio Wesleyan University which is located in its county seat. But hungry developers have recently seen to the destruction of all that. The urban sprawl of Columbus and Franklin County now reaches almost as far north as Galena, turning beautiful waterfront scenes into barren housing developments with few trees. There are, however, exceptions to the scourge of progress.

"Wallendon" is one of them. Hidden away in a forest on a 30-acre island in the reservoir, it is attached to the mainland road by a gated bridge, manned by plain-clothed guards. We reached a sign with an arrow beckoning, "This way to Wallendon," the home of Heinrich Wabstmann I suspected, which meant that we had reached the end of the line. We could follow the Andropov limousine no further without being observed.

A huge brick house rose in the distance beyond the gate, but there was nothing identifying its owner. The house was built like a 17th century castle, complete with a moat and towers in the fashion of a Prussian Junker estate. I had an inkling who the owner might be, but I wasn't sure what to do next. So I just waited long enough to be sure Picup's limo had passed through the gate. Then an idea came to me.

"Get out of the cab here; walk up to the gate like you're lost and ask them who lives here," I told the cab driver. "Tell them you're looking for the home of Heinrich Wabstmann. Remember everything they say. Then, if they offer to call the main house on your behalf, tell them not to do that, that you're with the county tax assessor's office, and that you'll be back, but you're being picked up by a county LLV down the road in a few minutes. Then leave immediately."

The gate was almost a quarter mile away, and it seemed to take my cab driver forever to accomplish this task and report back. He left the meter running. When he finally returned, he reported that the estate did indeed belong to Heinrich Wabstmann.

"But as I was leaving," he added, "I saw one of the guards pick up the phone even though I told them not to call the big house when they asked me if I wanted them to."

"OK, fine," I said. "Turn this car around and let's get out of here."

It seemed to take forever for him to get the boxy yellow cab turned around on the narrow road. I kept watching for the guards to come after us, but they didn't. On the trip back to Columbus, I called Rosanne again.

"Picup delivered Rolph to the Wabstmann estate."

"What? Where are you?"

"I'm in Galena, Ohio. It's like a little duchy belonging to Herr Heinrich Wabstmann. He lives on a beautiful tree-covered island. My guess is he employs half the people who live around here as security for his estate, gardeners, servants, mechanics for his cars, and political retainers."

"His place is really that big, huh? Well, God bless the rich and wealthy. What would we ever do if there were fewer of them around to throw the rest of us scraps?"

"His place is huge and very secure—guards everywhere."

"Well, where does that leave things, Winston?"

"I have no idea. Somehow, I've got to get Ronnie Herimus to have a look at Rolph, so he can tell me if Rolph was the man who visited him on the day Bruge Biliuss was murdered. I've got Rolph's picture in my phone but it's very poor quality."

"What do you suppose Rolph Van Heyde's connection is with Heinrich Wabsmann?"

"I have no idea. We'll have to figure that out soon, but first things first. Was Rolph the guy in Ronnie's kitchen? That's what I need to know now."

"Winston, I've got an idea how we can find that out."

CHAPTER TWENTY EIGHT

Picup put the cube of sugar between his front teeth, held it there with his lips open, raised a glass of black Russian tea, and sucked it through the sugar cube into his mouth, downing it with a gulp. "Ahh, that's how we used to do it in Moscow," he said, tearing the heel off the loaf of pumpernickel bread in front of him and chomping on it with his mouth open. Rosanne averted her eyes from the slovenly scene. To Anastasia, who was sitting next to Picup, the sight of him eating like a boor was quite normal.

We were sitting in the Russian Club, part of which is a delicatessen, on Rte. 161 near Linworth Road, to which we had brought the two Russians for lunch, hoping it would make Picup feel comfortable enough to discuss doing a favor for me. An added advantage of the place was that it was so far off the beaten track that we were the only ones there.

"I don't know, I don't know," Picup protested. "The whole thing doesn't sound quite kosher to me."

"What's to be kosher, Picup?" Ani upbraided him. "It's very simply—next time somebody from Wabstmann organization calls for pick up of man at the Sheraton, you call Winston and tell him what time they want you there. If you are in car at time with somebody else, you call me and tell me in Russian what time you are going to hotel. *Panemayish?* (You understand?)."

"Nothing bad will happen to you if you do this," I said. "Nobody will know but you and me, and maybe Anastasia. You don't have to do anything else."

"But what is the reason for this? Why do you want me to do it? The man won't know I've done it, yet it invades his privacy, doesn't it? Maybe I could lose my chauffeur's license by doing such a thing."

"As I told you before, Picup, I saw who the man was when you picked him up after running into me downtown. He owes one of my clients thousands of dollars, but he won't pay. He refuses to answer the door to his hotel room, and the sheriff's office does not have the time to stake out the hotel lobby so a summons can be served on him when they see him come down."

I was lying about this, but I went on with my lie, in too deep now to stop. "If he's not served with a summons here in Ohio, we'll never be able to start a collection action against him because there is no way of getting service when he goes back to his country. So, I need you to call next time you're going to make a pick-up of the man at the hotel for Wabstmann. That way, I can call the sheriff's office, and they can get a process server out there to serve him when he comes downstairs, and it won't be hit or miss. The process server will have his photograph with him." There, the little lie was complete.

"Well, what if they don't get him inside the hotel. Will the process server follow him outside to my car? Then I'll become involved, won't I, and what will I do?"

Ani slammed her hand down on the table hard enough to rattle Picup's tea glass. *"Ya ne dayu dermo, Picup!* (I don't give a shit, Picup!)," she shouted disgustedly. "You will simply put man in car, lock door and windows, and drive away!"

"Tei ne dayish dermo! (*You don't give a shit!) Hmph—easy for you to say! You won't be there." He reached for another chunk of black bread, but before he

could get it into his mouth, Ani slapped it out of his hand.

"Listen, Picup, it's time for you to—how they say it— to man up. Winston is our friend. How many times he has helped us? You can count? No. And, how many times he has helped us, no charge? You must do this little favor for him."

"Ok, ok, Anastasia, I will help him, but when I think of what he has done for us, especially the free things he has done, as you say, all I can think is that he brought your father here to Columbus to haunt us."

With that, Anastasia began to cry, as Picup continued remonstrating Igor's awfulness to her. Rosanne blushed deeply and asked me with her eyes to stop the two of them from carrying on, but there was no intervening in a fight between the two Ruskies. Instead, I got up to pay the bill. Our little Russian luncheon was over.

Two days later, Picup called to say he would be making a pick-up of Wabstmann's man at the Sheraton at 2:30 p.m. that day. I called Ronnie and told him to meet me in the Sheraton's lobby at 1:30. That would give us time to reconnoiter for a place to hide from which we could see Rolph pass by but he wouldn't notice us. We found a sofa near the exit partially hidden by a Japanese screen. Ronnie would be stationed there. I would hover near the cashier's desk, which was on the way out, and when Rolph came out of the elevator, I would "bump" into him precipitously and engage him in conversation long enough for Ronnie to get a good look at him.

At 2:25, the elevator doors opened and Rolph Van Heyde exited. "Rolph," I called, "is that you?"

Startled, he turned around, looking perturbed to have been noticed. When he saw me, he quickly pasted a smile over his look, and he walked over to me, greeting me, all hale and hearty. "I was going to call you," he said, "but I hadn't gotten around to it yet. Imagine, just running into you like this. Columbus must be as small a town as Bruges."

"Well, not quite, Rolph. What are you doing here anyways?"

"Business—I have business here. Really, I must go now, but give me your number and I will call. How is your friend—Rosanne, isn't it?" I gave him my office number because I wanted Marinda to be able to screen his call, and with that, he wheeled around and went out the hotel exit into the driveway beyond, where Picup was waiting for him in the limousine. Picup must have been happy to see there was no process server or deputy following him.

After the car pulled away, I signaled to Ronnie, and he emerged from behind the screen. He had a big smile on his face.

"Well? I said.

"That was him—the guy who visited me in my kitchen."

"His name is Rolph Van Heyde," I volunteered. He's from Bruges, Belgium, and he works for Pharmea Bruxelles, a subsidiary of Aiden Life. He's also a liar, which makes him a person of interest in your case, a person of very big interest.

"How do you know all this?" Ron asked.

"It's a long story. Rosanne and I met him in Belgium. He was actually following us around there. I'll tell you all about it later. But for now, we've got to find out more about why he's in Columbus."

"How are you going to do that, boss?"

"I think there's only one person who can give us information like that—Picup Andropov, but it's not going to be easy to get him to talk about Van Heyde."

"Maybe there are two people, boss. They must keep driving records for their car. What about his wife—what's her name? Ann?—maybe she could help."

"She's called Ani. It's short for Anastasia, and that's a great idea, Ron."

I called Anastasia Andropov and asked her if they kept records of the names of people they transported. She said they only had records of who hired them, not of the actual names of the people they drove around, unless those people were also the people who actually hired them. She confirmed that their biggest client was Aiden Life Pharmaceuticals, and that every time they drove for the company, there was an entry in the car service's records containing the date, the company's name, the pick-up point for each trip, and the destination accompanied by a mileage calculation.

"That's good, Ani. Is it ok if I come over and have a look at those records?"

"Sure, Winston," she said, "but not today. Come tomorrow. To find these records, it will take some time. Also, if you come tomorrow, Picup will be here. You can talk to him."

"Ok, Ani, thanks."

"And bring Rosanne, I'll make lunch—maybe some good borscht with roasted *kartofal*."

CHAPTER TWENTY NINE

"Picup, on the weekend you took the limo to the airport to pick up Igor, were you in the employ of Heinrich Wabstmann's organization?"

"Yes."

"For the entire weekend?"

"That's none of your business."

"The foreigner you are chauffeuring around now for Mr. Wabstmann, have you ever driven for him before this week? Were you driving for him also on that weekend?"

"Again, my friend—none of your business! Where would I be with the Picup Andropov Car Service if I informed on everyone I drove—where I took them, what they did—who was with them? No, no, and no!"

We were sitting in the Andropov living room— Rosanne, Anastasia, Picup and me—listening to Picup invoke a new legal concept, the "chauffeur-client privilege." Nobody can be more stubborn than a Russian. He simply wasn't going to give us any information. But as usual, Ani had other ideas.

"Winston, as I told you before, we keep record of everywhere we go by date, if we have customer we are driving on date in question. Maybe records could help, even though they don't say name of person actually in back seat. Let us look at records for date we went to airport to pick up my father. I look at whole weekend, ok?"

Ani spread the driving records out on the coffee table and leafed through them until she found the weekend her father was supposed to arrive at the airport. It was the same weekend Bruge Biliuss was murdered. Rosanne began examining the records with her accountant's eye, not knowing exactly what she was looking for.

"These records are very complete," she offered. "Oh, oh, oh, here it is, Winston. At 2:00 p.m. on the Saturday Igor Bashenko was supposed to arrive, we have the limo leaving the Sheraton Hotel and going to the airport. At 3:30 p.m., it goes to 3240 Montrose Avenue, here in Bexley."

"Yes, that's our address here," Ani said. "We came back from the airport with empty car that day. So we came home."

"You were pretty busy though," Rosanne opined. "Earlier that morning, around 8:00 a.m., the car went down to the Sheraton, and from there to 788 Langley in Whitehall; then back to the Sheraton. Then, between 10:00 a.m. and noon, it went to Vets Memorial Hall on West Broad. Then it went back to the Sheraton Hotel again. At 2:00 p.m. it left the Sheraton for the airport."

"Wait a minute, WAIT A MINUTE!" I said. "Did you say Langley in Whitehall? That's Ronnie Herimus' home address! Then, where did you say the car went?"

"To Vets Memorial on West Broad."

"And, how long was the car there?"

"About an hour and a half," Rosanne answered.

"And, then where did it go?"

"The Sheraton downtown."

"Picup," I demanded. "You were transporting the same man that morning that you were driving around the other day when you told me what time you would be at the Sheraton, weren't you? WEREN'T YOU?"

Picup shook his head no.

"Answer me!" I demanded. "Tell me exactly what you were doing at Vets Memorial that morning. The man's name was Rolph T. K. Van Heyde, wasn't it? Were you near a spray booth at Vets Memorial? You tell me exactly what you were doing at that time or I'm calling the police."

Picup looked up at me from the couch, like a wounded lamb. At this point, Ani did something I'd never seen her do before. She took Picup's side. Moving over to sit next to him, she said, "Picup doesn't know what our clients do. He just drives. Now, let's have some good borscht and *kartofel*."

Rosanne put her hand on my thigh to settle me down. "That's enough for now, Winston," she said in a low steady voice. "This may put Rolph at the scene of Bruge Biliuss' murder at the time it happened if he was Picup's customer on the trip to Vet's. Let's check the hotel registry of guests on that day for Rolph's name. If it's there, then I think you have enough to report all this to the police and to let them take it from there."

"No, Rosanne. There's a lot more to do, but maybe you're right. There may be nothing more we can get out of Picup."

"Will I have to talk with the police about this now?" Picup asked.

"Yes, Picup. You very definitely will," I answered, "and, it would be a good idea for you to think about it, and maybe even write out everything you did, saw and heard on that day before you say anything to them. And, if there's anything you feel you did that was wrong, you should consider invoking your Fifth Amendment right not to testify against yourself."

Picup shuddered and averted his eyes.

CHAPTER THIRTY

"I take my Fifth Amendment right not to answer under the Constitution of the United States," Picup insisted as formally as he could."

When the police showed up at her front door to speak with Picup, Ani called me and insisted that I represent him. She didn't realize that Rosanne and I had inspected the Sheraton's guest registry for Rolph's name and found that he was staying there on the date Picup drove the limo to the Sheraton; then to Ron Herimus's, and after that to Vets Memorial, where Bruge Biliuss was murdered.

Nor could she have imagined that Rosanne and I had reported this to the police. She also didn't know that we reported all the other facts we knew about Rolph Van Heyde—that he had followed us around Belgium, that he was friendly with Heinrich Wabstmann, that he had lied to us, that he had shown up at Ron Herimus's at 8:00 a.m. on the day Bruge Biliuss was murdered, that Ron had Sachmo's insulin syringes out in plain view when Rolph was in his kitchen and, that the syringe found at the scene of the murder came from the same lot as Sachmo's syringes.

I had a clear conscience about representing Picup in front of the police, because I did not suspect him of any wrong doing. He was merely a driver hired by Aiden Life Pharmaceuticals to transport Rolph Van Heyde around when he was in town, and he had no idea why his passenger might have directed him to go to Vets Memorial or anywhere else. Picup was just an honest hard working immigrant trying to make a living in the limousine business. But now, Detective Picard was bearing down on him mercilessly.

"The records indicate that Rolph T. K. Van Heyde was a guest at the Sheraton on the date you took your limo to Vets Memorial," Picard declared. "Did you drive Mr. Van Heyde to Vets Memorial on that date?"

"None of your business," Picup shot back—"Fifth Amendment."

"So, then, you know a man named Rolph Van Heyde. You know who he is."

"Same answer. I give you same answer—Fifth Amendment."

Detective Picard was getting frustrated. "Listen, Mr. Andropov, we haven't taken you into custody. That's why nobody has Mirandized you. We're simply asking you voluntarily to give us a few answers. We could, however, go over to the Sheraton, if you like, and find out when Mr. Van Heyde stayed there—you know it could have been more than twice—and then we could compare what we find with your driving records to see if Aiden Life Pharmaceuticals hired you for any of those dates. And, if the right match-up is there, we could come back and pick you up, and at that time you w*ould* be Mirandized, because you *would* be in custody."

"You mean to say that I am only talking to you voluntarily right now?" Picup inquired.

"That is correct," Picard answered.

With that, Picup got up from his chair; walked the police to the door and said good-by to them without another word. Ani followed him, exhorting him to let them stay and to answer Picard's questions, but he wouldn't hear of it.

"He's hiding something," Officer Shapiro opined when we got outside. "This is more than just stubborn Russian recalcitrance on his part."

"We're gonna have to put a tail on him," Picard said. "We'll follow him everywhere he goes for as long as that Belgian guy is checked in at the Sheraton. We're also gonna need an I. D. on the Belgian guy."

"Either Ronnie or I can give you that," I offered. Then I remembered I had a picture of Rolph on my phone from the first time I saw him outside the Sheraton.

"This photo will help," Picard said, "but I think we're still gonna need a personal I.D. The picture's too fuzzy."

The next day, Picard and Shapiro picked me up in an unmarked car and we drove down to stake out the auto entrance to the Sheraton. We watched Picup collect Rolph, and we sat there as the two of them talked together for almost five minutes before Rolph got into the limo and was driven away.

"Not exactly an impersonal chauffeur-client relationship," Shapiro remarked. "The two of them seem to know each other pretty well."

We followed the limo out to Wallendon in Galena, until we could go no further without being discovered. There, we waited for over an hour until Picup came out, leaving Van Heyde inside. As he drove away, Officer Shapiro said, "Why don't we keep following Andropov for a while, just for fun?"

We watched the limo drive back to the Sheraton and park in the auto pick-up area. Picup got out and went into the hotel. Half an hour later, he came out carrying a suitcase and a suit jacket and pants on a hanger, got in the limo, drove back to Wallendon, and, took the clothes inside. Obviously, Rolph was quitting the Sheraton to stay at Wallendon with Heinrich

Wabstmann. The question was why? Had Picup informed him of Picard's threat to compare his driving records with the dates of Rolph's stays at the Sheraton? Had Picup informed Rolph that he was now a person of interest to the Columbus Police Department? Was Picup more involved with Rolph, and for that matter, Aiden Life Pharmaceuticals, than a simple "see-nothing, hear-nothing, say-nothing" hired servant responsible for driving a limousine?

"Well, that's enough for today on this matter," Detective Picard announced. "There are only so many police resources we can devote to one case. As of now, I'm afraid we don't have much to go on. There's really no proof Rolph Van Heyde was anywhere near Bruge Biliuss on the day he was murdered—only inference, or even less, speculation. The only two people the evidence clearly places in the vicinity of Vets Memorial are Ron Herimus and Picup Andropov, and we really don't know what either of them was doing there. I'm afraid we're going to have to leave you to your own devices for a while on this one, counselor."

It was disappointing to see the police ducking out of the case, but I found Picard's statement very encouraging. He had evidence of a syringe with Ronnie's fingerprints on it inside the spray booth, which was the scene of the crime, and yet he was inferring that he really didn't *know* what Ron was doing at Vets Memorial on that day, stating merely that he was "in the vicinity." Maybe it meant I was making progress in Ronnie's case, at least with the police. It didn't mean, however, that I had enough to create reasonable doubt in the minds of a jury as to Ronnie's role in the murder. We had to find out more about what kept bringing Rolph to Columbus and what his true relationship with Heinrich Wabstmann was.

CHAPTER THIRTY ONE

It rained all night, with lightning and wind that wouldn't let up. The thunder didn't stop rolling until after 5:00 a.m. The atmosphere portended calamity, much like the "Ides of March" that Shakespeare wrote of in his play *Julius Caesar.* In the morning, as on every Thursday, the lithe cleaning lady let herself in at 9:00 a.m. to the Brewery District condominium, where Igor lived alone, now that Ida had rejoined her husband in Chicago. Little happened for half an hour or so as the pert little maid policed the kitchen, depositing the previous night's dishes in the dishwasher, the garbage in the trash compactor, scouring out the sink and wiping the counters clean of crumbs. But by 10:00 a.m., when Mr. Bashenko usually strode out of the bedroom, wearing his red silk bathrobe with paisley design, to say good morning and merrily tweak the young house cleaner's butt, as was his habit, he was still not up, and she began wondering if he was sick. So she went back into the bedroom to check on him.

He didn't wake up when she tapped his shoulder. He wasn't breathing. She called 911. The squad came, but they couldn't revive him. The police were called. Igor Bashenko was dead.

The maid called Anastasia Andropov immediately to notify her of her father's death, and Ani called me, carrying on like she'd forgotten how to speak English. Shrieking at the top of her voice, her words were coming more rapidly than the fastest tongue twister could possibly require. She was impossible to understand. All I could make out were the words "father, dead, apartment" and "police," and that I was to go over to Igor's place.

When I reached the condo, it was already taped off as a crime scene. The cleaning lady had just finished giving her written statement to the police and she was cowering on the couch waiting to be released. In her statement, she reported that there had been a strange noise as she entered the condo that morning, sort of like the rattle of more than one door closing from a build-up of air pressure when the main entrance door to an apartment or a house is slammed shut shaking other doors in the house, and it had surprised her because she never slammed the door when she entered. She was always careful to be quiet in case Mr. Bashenko was still sleeping. She would just close it behind her, carefully and quietly.

The coroner's people were busy supervising the bagging of the body. Officer Shapiro was on the phone with a .357 Magnum in a plastic bag sitting in front of him on the table. He was making arrangements to have the gun dusted for prints at the police station.

"Whose gun is that?" I asked.

"Don't know," Shapiro replied. "Do you know if Bashenko kept a gun in the house?"

"I don't know. Where'd you find it?"

"On the side table in his bedroom. There was a pencil in the barrel."

I went into the bedroom. Detective Picard was down on one knee looking at the carpet under the bed.

"What happened?" I asked.

"Don't know yet," Picard answered.

"Natural causes?" I asked.

"Don't know yet," Picard replied. "Coroner will have to tell us. I can't find any signs of someone being in this room with him. There are no wounds, no contusions, no signs of a scuffle, and no abrasions on the body, except for a few small dried blood stains at the back of his chin where he cut himself shaving."

"What about the gun?" I asked.

"Won't know anything about it until we dust it for prints, but there's no bullet wound, and it does not appear to have been fired."

The memory of watching the coroner fillet Bruge Biliuss in an antiseptic, white-tiled morgue with large aluminum body drawers along one wall and fluorescent lights overhead crept over me. Biliuss was somebody I never knew—a corpse. The impersonal attitude of the coroner still sent shivers up my spine. But this autopsy would be different.

Igor was the father of somebody I knew. He was my client. He was also an esteemed musician, an escaped refuge from a communist regime, an immigrant made good, a music maker par excellence, a lover not only of women, but of everyone, a giver of beauty, who left more with people than he took from them, a religious man with a conscience, albeit one afflicted with a bothersome mental illness. He was more than just a human being. He was a metaphor for much of humanity.

"Can't he just be taken to a hospital and evaluated there?" I asked this, thinking Anastasia might want him to receive a Jewish burial, even though she was completely secular, but knowing that at Jewish funerals a person must be buried with all their body parts. "There are no signs of criminal activity—forced entry or anything like that?" I added. "Does the coroner have to take him apart piece by piece?" My voice was cracking.

"You forget," Officer Shapiro reminded me. "There was an attempt on his life once before."

I had not forgotten that. But why would anyone want to take this man's life? Who hated him that much?—Joseph Dzugash? Ida? Picup? I doubted it. Where was the profit in it for anybody?

In any event, the coroner could wind up ruling that Igor Bashenko had died of natural causes. Many men died in their sixties, especially musicians with drug problems or past drug problems, and I really didn't know much about Igor's past personal life. I called Marinda at the office and told her to make a note to obtain a copy of the coroner's report when it came out.

"You're kidding," she said. "Igor Bashenko is dead? When?"

"This morning," I answered. "They found him at his condo."

"Was it a suicide?"

"What are you talking about, Marinda?" Why would Igor Bashenko commit suicide?"

"Well, do you think it had anything to do with his being relieved of his position as director of the symphony? That might be enough for me to kill myself if I were an important public figure like him. Stress can do strange things to people."

"I don't know, Marinda. At this time I haven't got the faintest idea what's going on with this thing. What's happening at the office this morning—anything?"

"No, not much—you had a call from somebody named Ralph Vanhigh."

"It's Rolph, Rolph Van Heyde—Rolph with an 'o'—he's foreign."

"Rolph, Ralph—it could have been Rolph. I don't know. He's not in our phone file," she replied. "Why would anyone want to be called Rolph? Isn't that when you throw up or something?"

"Did he leave a call back number?"

"No, he said he'd call you back at a later time."

I quickly hung up and pressed the Rosanne file in my cell phone contact list. "Rosanne, I've got two things to tell you, and you're not going to believe either of them. First, Igor Bashenko is dead. Second, Rolph Van Heyde called me today."

There was silence from the other end of the call. It lasted almost thirty seconds. Finally she spoke.

"Really!"

"Really what?" I asked eagerly.

"What happened?"

"To Bashenko?"

"Yes."

"Nobody knows yet."

"When's the funeral, and where?"

"I don't know. There has to be an autopsy first."

"How's Anastasia doing?"

"She's a mess."

More silence—then, "What did he want?"

"Who? Van Heyde?"

"Yes."

"I don't know. I wasn't there when he called. He's calling me back."

"What are you going to do when he calls back? Are you going to see him if he wants?"

"Do you think I should?"

"Yes, and I think I should be with you when you do. We should make it a purely social visit, play dumb, and just see what we can get out of him by listening—no probing into why he's here, no discussions about Aiden Life or his relationship with Wabstmann; nothing about Bruge Biliuss."

CHAPTER THIRTY TWO

Rolph did call back a day later, and he did propose getting together, but when I asked him if Rosanne could come, he hesitated. I told him it would really be hard for me not to bring her, since I'd told her I'd seen him and that after that he'd called me. So, reluctantly, he acceded to her coming along. I suggested we meet at Cap City Diner on Olentangy River Road.

"Is it a quiet place?" he asked. "I'd prefer a quiet out of the way place for our meeting."

So we wound up at The Top Steakhouse on Main Street, just outside Bexley. When we got there, the first thing I asked him was what he was doing in Columbus, Ohio. He said that his company, Pharmae Bruxelles was a subsidiary of Aiden Life Pharmaceuticals, and that he was in Columbus for a meeting with Aiden Life's CEO, Heinrich Wabstmann.

"You see, in essence, I work for Mr. Wabstmann, sometimes doing special projects for him. In fact, that's why I wanted to have dinner with you tonight."

"Tell me," I said, "what is the exact nature of your relationship with Wabstmann?"

"I am his cousin, a distant cousin, but nonetheless, his cousin. When Germany invaded Belgium during World War II, my father, who was the son of his father's brother, was removed to Berlin with our entire family to live with Heinrich's family."

"And now you work for him?"

"I have worked for him for twenty-five years. He trusts me because I am family."

"So then, as you said earlier," I continued, "our dinner tonight is not just a little social get-together because I happened to bump into you after the days we spent with each other in Europe. You're actually on a special project for Heinrich Wabstmann."

"That is correct. You see, Heinrich would like to settle the Bashenko suit with you for a reasonable amount, to be negotiated, of course, but something well north of the remainder of Bashenko's contract with the Columbus Symphony. Everything is to be kept very confidential, with not even a mention of any settlement in the dismissal order or, elsewhere. In return, all he requires from you is a little cooperation."

"Doesn't he know that Igor Bashenko is deceased?" Rosanne asked.

Rolph seemed taken by surprise, "No, apparently not. When did this happen?"

"Yesterday, it hasn't made the papers yet. The police are currently looking into the matter because of the previous attempt on his life," I volunteered. "The death may have been from natural causes but the police are checking for foul play. It also may have been a suicide."

"I must report this to Mr. Wabstmann immediately," Rolph replied, but I am pretty certain it will not change the offer I've made. He can simply settle with Bashenko's estate. Can he not? You're a lawyer and you know about things like that. Don't you?"

"And what kind of cooperation does he require from me to go forward with such a settlement?" I asked

"He wants to know everything you know about the murder of Bruge Biliuss," Rolph answered, "things like the conclusions of the coroner in the autopsy report; like what you know about the syringe that was found next to Biliuss' body; and things like what Geertje Biliuss told you.

"How does he know I ever spoke to Geertje Biliuss?"

"Oh, he knows, not only that, but he knows that your friend Rosanne here spoke to her alone, without you."

"But how does he know that?"

Rolph's look became ominous. He began fidgeting with his silverware, punching the tip of his fork down into the table cloth.

"Oh, please, Mr. Barchrist, I know that you've followed me out to Wallendon twice—once even with the police—and so does Heinrich, and you knew that I was following you around in Belgium. But, I suppose what they say is true, 'if it's good for the goose, it's good for the gander,' eh? Let's just be honest with each other. Shall we?" He looked threateningly at Rosanne.

"How does he know I know anything at all about the murder of Bruge Biliuss?"

"You're on record as his attorney, Mr. Barchrist, and anyway, maybe somebody has been following you around here in Columbus too."

I was no longer looking forward to the Porterhouse steak I had planned on ordering tonight, with a twice-baked cheese potato, onion rings, shrimp on ice, a salad and a bottle of wine. The whole conversation had made me very un-hungry. In fact, I thought I might be getting sick. Rosanne was just downright scared from knowing she'd been followed in Belgium, and that she was heavily involved in a matter she did not understand.

"Why does Heinrich Wabstmann require all this information about the murder of Bruge Biliuss?" I asked.

"He just does, Winston, and I'm afraid that's none of your affair."

"In other words, he wants to know my entire defense for Ron Herimus. He wants what we call my entire 'attorney's work product' in the Herimus case. No, I don't think so. In the first place, all that is privileged information, and in the second place, I think the Bar Association could take my license from me if I divulged it."

Van Heyde smirked, "Oh, but think, Winston, think how worthwhile it would be for you. Not only would you make a nice percentage off what will be a fat settlement in the Igor Bashenko case, now with his estate, of course, but think how worthwhile Mr. Wabstmann could make your cooperation with him on the Biliuss matter, monetarily of course, through both the value of the case settlement and the settlement of your attorney fees."

I looked at Rosanne, and she gave me a knowing look back. "No. no, and NO, Mr. Van Heyde," I said.

Van Heyde's mood darkened even more. "Well, Mr. Barchrist, I think you are going to regret your decision on this. Why don't you take one or two days to think about it? In the meantime, I'll tell the boss about Mr. Bashenko's untimely demise and see if that has any effect on things."

"Why would that affect anything?" Rosanne asked.

"Oh, I don't know," Van Heyde replied. "Maybe because Aiden Life is the biggest continuing client of the Picup Andropov Car Service, maybe because Picup Andropov hated his father-in-law so much, or maybe just because it brings an end to the ongoing embarrassment Bashenko has caused the Symphony Board. Some money may have to be paid to his estate, but he'll never have to be re-employed." With that, he pushed his chair away from the table and departed, leaving the bill for his drinks for me to settle.

"What do you suppose he meant by all that?" Rosanne asked.

"I don't know, Rosanne, but one thing's for certain. We should stay away from that man. I think that it's not

Heinrich Wabstmann who wants to know all about what I know about the Bruge Biliuss case, but rather Rolph Van Heyde who wants to know."

Before we could get up, my cell rang. It was Marinda.

"I'm at the office working late tonight. Detective Picard called with the preliminary conclusions of the coroner on Mr. Bashenko," she reported, "death from *unnatural* causes, a broken hyoid bone in the throat. I thought you would want to know right away."

CHAPTER THIRTY THREE

"Often impetuous, often contrite, but always loved—that was Igor Bashenko," the eulogy began. "He brought beauty into the lives of everyone."

Picup scoffed. "That rabbi never knew him. How he can presume to say anything about your father is beyond me," he whispered to Anastasia. Anastasia grimaced. She knew Picup wasn't perturbed with the rabbi. He was angry with Igor, and at the public outpouring of sympathy on his behalf at his memorial service. To Picup, Igor had brought nothing but the curse of his disease into his life with Anastasia, and Igor had heaped nothing but humiliation on both of them.

The public celebration of the life of Igor Bashenko was held inside the glass atrium at the Ohio Theater, because it was the home of the Columbus Symphony Orchestra. Rosanne and I were in attendance, standing next to the Andropovs, with almost 1000 people behind us. There were no seats. Everyone was standing. The entire Columbus Symphony board of trustees, sans Heinrich Wabstmann, was present. The mayor and his staff were also present. The Ohio Arts Council was represented. The Columbus Cultural Arts Center was represented. Important dignitaries from the Columbus Association for Performing Arts (CAPA) were there. The entire roster of Ballet Met was present, along with the players of the Columbus Chamber Orchestra and a contingent from the Ohio State University, including the Music Director of the Ohio State Buckeye Band.

The president of the Columbus Federation of Musicians walked in, along with the national president of the American Federation of Musicians from New York. Countless players from the Trans-Siberian Orchestra came all the way from California to be there. The Columbus Symphony, led by the beautiful, but now very emotional, Concertmaster Miriam Jaspers, offered three selections of very sad music in homage to their former maestro: Shostakovich's *Largo* from *Symphony No. 5*; *Cantus in Memory of Benjamin Britton*; and, *Der Leiermann* from Shubert's *Die Winterreise.* Almost nobody left with dry eyes.

Toward the end of the program, the door leading to the symphony practice room opened at the back of the atrium revealing Janic Vadea standing there with his hands on his hips staring out at the crowd. Next to him, stood Rolph Van Heyde. Neither man showed any emotion. I had not yet given Van Heyde my final answer to the proposition he made to me on behalf of Heinrich Wabstmann, but I had decided my answer was still going to be "no."

Suddenly, Officer Shapiro and Detective Picard appeared at the symphony practice room door and began talking to Van Heyde. Van Heyde became animated. Vadea stepped back into the shadowy hallway leading to the practice room and closed the door, leaving Van Heyde outside to deal with the two policemen. Watching over my shoulder as this scene unfolded, I couldn't see everything that was going on, so I decided to make my way toward Rolph and the cops through the crowd and appear to "bump" into them socially. I told Rosanne to wait for me and that I'd be back. But I was unable to reach them before they left.

Shapiro and Picard were leading Van Heyde out of the building. My curiosity overwhelmed me. Were my eyes deceiving me or did they have Rolph in handcuffs? I picked up my pace, bumping into people and excusing myself as I cut through the crowd.

When I reached them, before I could say anything, Rolph said, "Hello, Mr. Barchrist. Do you remember me telling you in Bruges that if I was ever in Columbus and needed a lawyer, I'd call on you? Well, now is that time. It appears I'm being arrested and I need you."

"Shapiro," I asked, "Is that true? Are you arresting him?"

"Yah, its true, counselor, but what's going on here? First, you give us all that background information on this guy and now he wants you to be his lawyer? I don't get it."

"That's enough, Shapiro," Picard admonished, "no more talking, officer. Please."

Rolph glared at me. "What did you tell them?" he demanded.

"What's he being arrested for?" I asked.

Van Heyde replied. "For the murder of Igor Bashenko! At least, that's what they're telling me. I didn't even know Igor Bashenko. Can you believe it?"

"What? Igor Bashenko?" Rolph's response flummoxed me. For one thing, if Rolph Van Heyde didn't even know Igor Bashenko, what was he doing at his funeral? Secondly, all the information I had given to the police about Van Heyde pointed to his possible involvement in the death of Bruge Biliuss, not Igor Bashenko. Picard picked up on the questioning look that must have spread over my face.

"Take it easy, Mr. Barchrist," he said. "Everything will become apparent to you in due course."

"Well, I'm certainly not going to comply with the request of Mr. Van Heyde here to be his lawyer, but as you may or may not know, I do, did, represent Igor Bashenko, specifically in a civil matter he had commenced against Heinrich Wabstmann and others, and the discovery in that case has unearthed the fact that Mr. Van Heyde was Mr. Wabstmann's close friend. Indeed, Mr. Van Heyde later admitted to me that he was Mr. Wabstmann's trusted employee of twenty-five years, and also a distant member of his family. I would like to accompany you to the station, to learn more about Mr. Van Heyde's relationship to Mr. Bashenko. Maybe he too should be a defendant in the Bashenko suit against Wabstmann. Indeed, he has made some very curious statements to me about the effects Mr. Bashenko's death might have on the settlement of the lawsuit between Messrs. Bashenko and Wabstmann"

"And we would like to have you come along," Picard indicated in a welcoming voice, "so that we might learn what you uncovered about Mr. Van Heyde during your discovery in that civil suit."

"May I bring my friend Rosanne?" I asked.

"No, I'm afraid not," Picard said. "We're probably violating some rule or other even by letting you come along. You'll have to call her on your cell and tell her to leave without you."

And, that's what I did. When we arrived at the station, while the intake officers were busy slating Van Heyde, Picard began explaining to me what was going on. We wouldn't be able to see Van Heyde again for a couple of hours until they were finished inventorying his possessions, taking his mug shots, fingerprinting him, assigning him his jail clothes and settling him into his cell. So Picard took the opportunity to bring me up to speed on what the Department had been doing in Ronnie Herimus's case.

He explained that the coroner had determined that Bruge Biliuss had died from his smashed hyoid bone *before* the overdose of insulin that had been injected into him could have killed him. Thus, unless Ron was the one who could have broken the hyoid, he was no longer under suspicion because it was doubtful he could have performed that act on Biliuss's hyoid in the manner it was done—cleanly with no damage to the other tissues of the neck. The coroner determined that the bulk of the insulin received by Biliuss had remained close to the injection site. The only explanation for this was that Biliuss was dead before it was injected; his heart had stopped beating; and, thus, there was no means of pumping the insulin through his body in his bloodstream. There were no traces of insulin in his heart, either from the systolic or the diastolic functions of his heartbeat. The coroner had also concluded that Biliuss' hyoid bone had been very carefully broken, almost surgically, without any signs of a struggle or rough strangulation.

So why wasn't Ronnie also suspected of smashing Biliuss's hyoid bone? Picard revealed the CDP had been in close touch with the Department of Police Inspection in Tourhout, Belgium, ever since Rosanne and I told them that Rolph had been following us around Belgium, and that Niels Blenker, with whom we had met for lunch there, had, like Bruge Biliuss, died of a broken hyoid bone. The Touhout police reported for a long time, however, that they suspected Blenker's work associate, Felix de Wolff, of murdering Blenker, because a glass of milk was found next to Blenker's body with de Wolff's fingerprints on it, and Blenker's lips were smeared with the milk. Blenker was known to love milk, and de Wolff was known to bring him glasses of it fresh from the cows on his family's farm where he lived.

This time, however, the milk was laced with Tremetol, a poison from a plant known as the White Sanicle. In the early Nineteenth century, thousands had died from something called the Milk Sickness because cows had eaten the White Sanicle and were absorbing Tremetol from the plant into their systems. In the days before pasteurization, the toxin was absorbed into the cow's milk and thereby transferred to humans who died. De Wolff protested that all the milk from his farm was pasteurized. But there was no way to prove the milk in this particular glass had been pasteurized. De Wolff also argued he had no motive for killing Blenker.

The investigation revealed that Rolph Van Heyde, who in addition to working at Pharmae Bruxelles, was known to be a corporate compliance officer for the parent company, Aiden Life, had learned Blenker had eaten lunch with Rosanne and me, and that Van Heyde also suspected Niels Blenker may have put de Wolff on to talking to Rosanne and me about the corporate secrets of Aiden Life Pharmaceuticals. De Wolff vehemently denied ever talking to us, but as the theory of the Tourhout police goes, de Wolff, who in truth had talked to us, needed to shut Blenker up before Blenker admitted to Van Heyde that he had given de Wolff our phone number in Bruges and told him to call us. Everyone knew the penalty at Phamea Bruxelles for talking to outsiders about company business was the corporate death penalty, ie.—discharge. So, de Wolff did have a motive. He didn't want Van Heyde to be able to prove Blenker had put him in contact with Rosanne and me.

But when the coroner in Touhout announced that the true cause of Blenker's death was a broken hyoid, not the poisoned milk, the theory that de Wollf had killed Blenker began to fall apart. The only person other than de Wolff known to have been in the lab with Blenker on the day he died was Van Heyde, who was probably there questioning Blenker about the whole matter of de Wolff's talking to us. In fact, Van Heyde was now wanted by the Touhout police for questioning. Picard finished his description of what happened in Tourhout by emphasizing that the coroner there had concluded, like the coroner in Columbus, that Blenker's hyoid bone had been very carefully broken, almost surgically, without any signs of rough strangulation, as was the case with Biliuss's hyoid bone. In other words, it was as if the same perpetrator had done both jobs, even though one happened in Belgium and the other in Columbus, Ohio.

"I'm told by both coroners," Picard added, "that it's rare and very unusual to find the hyoid bone snapped without any other damage to the neck.

"That brings us to Igor Bashenko's case," Picard continued. "There are three things about all of these crimes that are the same. First, there's always something at the scene that leads the investigator away from the true cause of death—in the Biliuss case it was the syringe; in the Blenker case it was the empty glass of milk. Secondly, the cause of death is the same—a broken hyoid, and thirdly, the killer always makes a clean job of breaking this bone without any other signs of strangulation about the neck."

"I understand that at the scene of Biliuss's death the misleading clue was the broken syringe with Ron Herimus' prints on it, and at the scene of Blenker's death, it was the glass of milk with de Wolff's prints on it," I said. "But what was the misleading clue left in Igor's condominium?"

"Ah, didn't anyone tell you?" Picard replied. "In Bashenko's condo, we found a .357 Magnum with the fingerprints of Picup Andropov all over it. There was no bullet wound, of course, but when we checked, a gun Anastasia Andropov said was normally kept in their limo was missing."

"Thus, pointing you toward Picup Andropov as the killer," I said, "but in the first two cases you've got something tying Van Heyde to the murder scenes. With Biliuss, there's the evidence, circumstantial though it may be, that on the morning of the murder, Picup Andropov drove Rolph Van Heyde to Vet's Memorial where Biliuss was murdered. In the Blenker case, there are facts which also place Van Heyde at the scene of the crime—the Pharmae Bruxelles lab that is—around the time of the murder. But there's nothing showing that Rolph was in Bashenko's condo on the morning he was murdered."

Picard smiled. "Oh but there is. The maid said that as she entered that morning, she heard a door rattle and slam, possibly the back door, as she closed the front door behind her. She never slammed the front door through which she came because she didn't want to wake up Igor if he was sleeping. We found a single print on the knob of the back door. Our good friends at Interpol were kind enough to confirm that the print belonged to one Rolph T. K. Van Heyde of Bruges, Belgium."

"So, then, are you charging Van Heyde with all three murders?"

"No, only with the murder of Igor Bashenko right now. Blenker's murder occurred outside our jurisdiction. The Belgians will have to extradite him. As for the murder of Bruge Biliuss, the charges against Ron Herimus will be dropped, but we're not charging Rolph on that one *yet*, because there's really no hard proof he was at Vet's Memorial on the morning of the killing. Yes, he was in Columbus at the Sheraton on that day. Yes, Ron Herimus has identified him as the man who came to his house on the morning of Biliuss's death, and yes, Picup Andropov's records indicate Picup took the limousine to Vet's Memorial that morning. But Mr. Andropov refuses to talk to us. He won't say that he drove Van Heyde to Vet's Memorial.

He won't say who he drove there. So we can't quite put the stopper in that bottle yet."

CHAPTER THIRTY FOUR

"The evidence—one fingerprint matched against Interpol's 1987 records—is simply not good enough to prove beyond a reasonable doubt that my client is guilty of murder. It's really not even enough evidence to arrest on," bellowed Gabe Whittisack, the attorney whom Heinrich Wabstmann had hired to defend Rolph Van Heyde. "We propose that the defendant be released on his own recognizance pending trial."

"Your honor, this man is from Belgium. How will we regain custody of him if he runs back there? I should think the appropriate order would be either no bail at all or bail at five million dollars." We were sitting in the courtroom at Rolph's arraignment—Anastasia, Ronnie, Rosanne and I. Strangely, Heinrich Wabstmann was also present, sitting alone at the rear of the room. Rolph was in the prisoner's dock, wearing orange overalls and chains. He had already pled not guilty. He had also refused to waive his right to a speedy trial. Now the question of his bail was being considered.

"Your honor, this man is the cousin of Mr. Heinrich Wabstmann," Whittisack continued, looking around toward the back of the room, "You know, the CEO of Aiden Life Pharmaceuticals?"

"Yes, yes, of course," answered the judge.

"Mr. Van Heyde is currently residing in Mr. Wabstmann's home. It is an estate on an island at Hoover Reservoir. The court could place him under house arrest there—you know, put a radio band around his ankle, and if he left the island it would only be with the assent of the police and he would have to be accompanied by an officer of the police department, the probation department or the court."

"Your Honor, we propose bail of five million dollars," the prosecutor again insisted.

The judge looked back at Heinrich Wabstmann who discretely shook his head "no."

"House arrest is appropriate here," Whittisack repeated, and Mr. Wabstmann could dedicate one of his bodyguards to accompany the prisoner at all times if he goes off the premises. The judge again looked to the back of the courtroom where Wabstmann was sitting. This time Wabstmann almost imperceptibly shook his head "yes"

"Alright, then," said the judge, "that's how it shall be—house arrest at the estate of Heinrich Wabstmann, supervised by the Department of Corrections. Additionally, one of Mr. Wabstmann's guards shall be deputized and dedicated to watching the defendant."

That was the last I saw of Rolph Van Heyde until three weeks later when he suddenly showed up at my office. He wore a radio shackle around his ankle and a guard whom Wabstmann had provided was with him. As he looked around my shabby office over the Dairy Mart store, I could see he was having trouble believing that this could be the professional dwelling of an attorney. Then Gabe Whittisack arrived.

"We have taken the liberty of coming here unannounced in an effort to prepare Mr. Van Heyde's defense," Gabe began. "We made no appointment in advance because we weren't sure you would see us. If you have someone else coming, or something else scheduled for this time slot, we will be happy to wait outside for you." He cast an unwelcoming eye toward my meager waiting room. "At the time of Mr. Van

Heyde's arrest for the murder of Igor Bashenko, one of the officers involved mentioned that you had given the police what they called 'background information' on my client," Gabe continued. "This was very surprising to him. We're here to find out what that was all about. What sort of background information did you give the police, and when?"

At this point, I realized that I was going to be called as a witness at Rolph's trial, either by the prosecution or by the defense, so I made a decision. "Yes, I will cooperate with you," I said, "and this is as good a time as any for us to talk. There's only one thing. Will you allow me to record our conversation?"

"Yes, Mr. Barchrist," Whittisack replied, "it's the least we can do in return for your cooperation."

So, Marinda brought in a recorder; turned it on; and Whittisack began. "Well, Mr. Barchrist, so what's it all about? When did you talk to the police about my client; and what sort of background did you give them that led to his arrest for Mr. Bashenko's murder?"

"None, so far as I know," I began. "I talked to the police sometime around—let me think—it would have been around two weeks after I had taken Mr. Vadea's deposition in Igor Bashenko's civil suit against Heinreich Wabstmann, so that would have been a little over a month ago from today. The conversation was actually in reference to charges that had been filed against Mr. Ronald Herimus whom I am defending for the murder of a body builder named Bruge Biliuss. You may have seen references to the case in the papers. Mr. Biliuss was from Belgium and Mr. Herimus was competing against him in the Arnold Schwarzenegger body building competition."

"Yes, I've heard of that case," Whittisack allowed.

"Anyway," I continued, "there was an empty insulin syringe found at the scene of the crime which implicated Mr. Herimus because his fingerprints were all over it. But the coroner had also determined that Mr. Biliuss' hyoid bone had been carefully and meticulously broken, without leaving any evidence of a struggle on his body. Do you know what the hyoid bone is?"

"Yes," Whittisack replied.

"OK, then, so it was either the broken hyoid, or insulin poisoning, that caused Biliuss's death. Insulin poisoning pointed to my client, Mr. Herimus, but the existence of a broken hyoid pointed to someone else. I only had a few other facts to work with at the time: 1) Mr. Herimus was giving insulin injections to a cat that lived with him; 2) he kept the preloaded syringes for these injections on his kitchen counter; 3) the lot number of these syringes matched that of the syringe found at the scene of the crime; 4) on the morning of the murder, Mr. Herimus had a visitor claiming to represent a pharmaceutical company, who, with the promise of an endorsement contract, tried to convince Ron to take the steroid manufactured by the company he represented. The visitor also told Mr. Herimus that Mr. Biliuss had refused to take this steroid.

"I told the police that since this evidence had not left me much with which to defend Mr. Herimus, I decided to go to Belgium with my friend Rosanne Harmon and attempt to find out more about Mr. Biliuss by talking to his wife.

"I further reported that while we were in Belgium, we learned that Mr. Biliuss had sensitive proprietary information about a secret project he had worked on as an employee of Pharmae Buxelles, a subsidiary of the Aiden Life Pharmaceutical Company. I told them that by what seemed like pure chance, we also met Mr. Van Heyde in Belgium; that we became friends with him there; and, that Mr. Van Heyde told us he'd never been to Columbus, Ohio, when in fact, he had. Later, I discovered that Mr. Van Heyde was following us around Belgium, and that he, like Mr. Biliuss, also worked for Pharmae Bruxelles. I told Detective Picard that Mr. Van Heyde followed us when we contacted Mr. Biliuss' wife twice, and that he followed us to the facility of Pharmae Bruxelles in Tourhout, Belgium, where we interviewed Mr. Niels Blenker, a co-worker of Mr. Biliuss's who had worked on the same secret project with him. Mr. Blenker told us that both men had proprietary information about the drug that was the subject of the project; and that both took the company's steroid to aid in their body building process. It turned out that also both men had been rewarded by the company for their efforts on the project, Mr. Biliuss with a trip to the United States to compete in the Schwarzenegger competition, where he would be taking steroids manufactured by Pharmae Bruxelles, and Mr. Blenker with a gym membership for five years in Belgium. I further informed the Columbus Police that a day or two after we talked to Mr. Blenker, he was found dead—dead, according to the Tourhout coroner, as I learned later, of a meticulously snapped hyoid."

"Just as an aside, I have learned since talking to the Columbus Police that they followed up on the Blenker death with the Touhout police commission, and that they learned that, as in the case of Mr. Biliuss, there was also evidence in the Blenker case, which I myself never learned of but was later told about, pointing to another cause of death—a glass of poisoned milk with the fingerprints of one of Mr. Blenker's co-workers all over it. Apparently, the Columbus Police discovered that after I talked to them about Mr. Van Heyde.

"In any event, I further told the Columbus Police that while in Belgium, we also discovered that Mr. Van Heyde knew, or had some sort of relationship with

Heinrich Wabstmann. We learned this from Mr. Van Heyde himself.

"Then, suddenly, Mr. Van Heyde showed up in Columbus, and, as things turned out, I learned he was being chauffeured around by my client, Picup Andropov, who is a regular driver for Mr. Wabstmann on much of his company's business, driving company visitors around town to the airport and such. I reported this to the police, but please note that Andropov never told me he'd been a driver for Mr. Van Heyde. I learned that serendipitously when I happened to see Picup pick up Mr. Van Heyde at the Sheraton. I then followed them to Mr. Wabstmann's castle, or estate, or whatever you want to call it.

"By this time, I was getting really nosey about Mr. Van Heyde, because I was suspecting him of maybe having some sort of involvement in the murder of Mr. Biliuss. I arranged to have Mr. Herimus surreptitiously view Mr. Van Heyde in the lobby of the Sheraton. Mr. Herimus confirmed that Mr. Van Heyde was the man who had visited him in his kitchen on the morning Mr. Biliuss was murdered. So Van Heyde had lied. He had been in Columbus before we met him in Belgium. Not only that, but he could have easily removed one of the insulin syringes from Mr. Herimus' kitchen if he was there and used it in the murder of Bruge Biliuss. I told the police all about this, and all about my suspicions.

"Could Picup Andropov also have driven Mr. Van Heyde to Mr. Herimus's house on that day," I wondered. "After all, he seemed to be the driver whom Mr. Wabstmann supplied for him whenever he was in Columbus.

"The Andropov's limousine trip records showed that Picup had driven the limousine from the Sheraton Hotel to the address of Ronald Herimus on the morning of the Biliuss murder, and that later that same morning, Picup had come back to the Sheraton, and then driven from there out to Vet's Memorial, where Biliuss was actually murdered. The Sheraton's guest records showed that Mr. Van Heyde was a guest at the Sheraton on that day. It was when I saw the driving records for the limo that I decided to go to the police and tell them everything I have just related to you."

Whittisack looked puzzled. Van Heyde looked uncomfortable. He squirmed in his chair and began to speak. "I know how this makes things look, but I can ex—"

Whittisack cut him off. "You don't have to explain anything at this point, and my advice to you is not to say anything."

"—But there—"

"No," said Whittisack, "Don't say anything!" Then he turned to me. "Mr. Barchrist, taking into account everything you've told the police, and assuming its truth, I fail to see how any of it implicates my client in the murder of Igor Bashenko."

"I don't see how it does either, Mr. Whittisack. But that's all I told them, and I would testify to that if I had to."

Rolph then asked if he and his lawyer could step outside for a moment to confer. When they returned, Whittisack asked me if I knew of anything that established that Van Heyde was ever at the scene of Igor's murder. "No," I answered, "not at the scene of the murder of Igor Bashenko."

"Well, do you have any evidence he was,"—then he caught himself up short and said, "—oh, well, never mind—nothing else."

"His story makes it look like I killed Bruge Biliuss and Niels Blenker," Van Heyde suddenly blurted, "and I don' like it because that's not true!."

Whittisack, probably more out of client relations than anything else, then decided to go ahead with the question he'd stopped himself from asking. "Mr. Barchrist," he said, "tell me, am I correct in stating that there was nothing you told the police that indicated any direct evidence that Rolph Van Heyde was ever at the scene of the Biliuss or the Blenker murders?"

"That's correct, sir."

"It's all circumstantial, isn't?"

"Yes."

"And tell me, is there any direct evidence within your personal knowledge that places my client at the scene of Mr. Bashenko's murder?"

"No."

CHAPTER THIRTY FIVE

The last concert of the season was a disheartening affair, especially for the players. It was dedicated to Igor Bashenko. Five months had elapsed since Janic Vadea had taken over as maestro, but only one month had gone by since Bashenko's murder. Nobody had forgotten it. So, when Ida Dzugash showed up for the final performance of the season, certain people were flabbergasted, including me. I couldn't believe my eyes when I saw her entering the Ohio Theater.

What was she doing back in Columbus? With the arrest of Rolph Van Heyde, the police had terminated their investigation of Joseph Dzygash as a person of interest in Igor's murder. So her presence in town could not have been associated with any police actions concerning Dzugash. Dzugash had an air-tight alibi anyway. He was able to prove that on the night Igor Bashenko was murdered, he was in Chicago at a "Texas Holdem" poker tournament where he won $6000.00.

So why had Ida Dzugash come back to Columbus? Things became more confusing a week later when the *Dispatch*'s social page published a piece about the annual Columbus Symphony Ball containing Ida's photograph. The Columbus Symphony Ball is the orchestra's largest, fund-raising, social event. There was Ida, smiling almost cheek-to-cheek with Janic Vadea out the window of a black limousine. The reference under the picture read, "Music Director Janic Vadea with his "good friend," Ida Dzugash, leaving the ball, and there was an accompanying article recounting the maestro's off-again, on-again career with the symphony over the past three years. More interesting than the article, at least to me, was the chrome shield with letters etched in it on the expanded doorpost between the front and back seats of the car in which Vadea and Ida were sitting. Under magnification, I could see the letters "PACS" in the news photograph. It was the logo of the Picup Andropov Car Service that was very familiar to me. Further scrutiny revealed that the grainy image in the portion of the front window on the driver's side that was in the photograph was the back of Picup's head wearing his signature Russian cap. The car was the Picup Andropov limousine, but what was Picup doing chauffeuring Ida Dzugash, whom he hated, around? And, where was the jealous Joseph Dzugash? There was no sign of him.

It was none of my business but curiosity overwhelmed me. So I hired Trudy Fischel to use her computer expertise for a check of the domestic court docket of Cook County, Illinois, which bore out what I suspected was going to happen sooner or later. Ida and Joseph had filed for divorce. For a hundred dollars more, Trudy cracked Visa's credit card records which revealed what Ida had recently spent her money on in Columbus. Trudy called back a day later.

"Wallah, she's still here and she's staying at the Marriott Residence Inn out by the airport," Trudy reported. "It's one of those extended stay hotels." .

I thought about calling Ida there but decided it would be too easy for her just to avoid me if I did. So I drove out to the Marriott and appeared at her door. The best description of her face when she opened the door, was absolute shock. Obviously not expecting a visitor, she'd done little at this hour of the morning to ready herself for her day, but she still looked trim and well developed in all the right places. I had forgotten what an elegant and inviting woman plastic surgery had made of her. The tiny hint of an accent in her voice was still seductive.

"What is your purpose in calling on me?" she demanded. "I understand the police have arrested somebody in connection with Igor's murder. So what is it you want from me, and why couldn't you have used the phone instead of coming in person?"

"How did you learn that an arrest had been made?" I asked.

"Oh, I have my ways of keeping up on what goes on in Columbus."

"And how might that be?" I asked. "Could it have been through, as the *Dispatch* describes him, your new 'good friend,' Janic Vadea?"

"What is it to you if Janic is my friend? For all you know, we could have been friends while I was still living here. Igor never bothered to pay enough attention to me to notice. So how would you know? More importantly, why would you care?"

"So, it was Janic Vadea who told you an arrest had been made in connection with Igor's murder."

Yes, Janic told me they had arrested Rolph—so what?"

"Oh, so you know Rolph Van Heyde?" I said

"Well, I don't really know him," she insisted, "I—"

"Well, you seem to know him well enough to refer to him by his first name."

"—know who he is, no."

"And who is he?" I asked.

Her face grew red; her enticing black eyes narrowed; and she began showing the furry for which I remembered her.

"Listen, Mr. Barchrist, I don't know why you're here, but I don't appreciate your cross examining me."

"I'd just like to know what you know about Rolph Van Heyde," I replied. "May I come in?'

"All I know is he's Janic's friend, and no, you may not come in," she said.

"Friend!" I retorted, not associate or acquaintance, "But you call him Janic's friend? Let me ask again. Did you know him? Have you ever spoken with him?"

"I don't have to answer your questions, Mr. Barchrist!"

I decided to try to inflame her even more in the hopes she would accidently blurt out something about Rolph and his relationship with Vadea that she was trying to hide. So I said, "Tell me, Ida, did you enjoy riding in the Andropov's limousine *again*. That was Picup driving, wasn't it? I'm sure you remember him. So what's going on?"

She shoved me back on my heels and then she slammed the door in my face. Clearly there was no point in pursuing her further about anything. Our conversation strongly hinted, however, that she not only knew Rolph Van Heyde, but that she may have even spoken with him. The only way to find out was to ask Rolph himself. I had cooperated in answering his questions, or the questions of his attorney, that is. Maybe now was the time for him to return the favor by answering questions I had about his relationship with Ida Dzugash.

CHAPTER THIRTY SIX

Wallendon was impressive from the road, which was the only location from which I'd seen it in the past, but the interior of the house was like a palace. After crossing the bridge from the mainland onto the island, the visitor came to a stream outside a large wall in front of the house with a draw bridge that could be pulled up against the wall by a chain as if the stream were a moat. Beyond the moat, was a courtyard of European paving stones leading to a covered entrance under which a car could draw up to disembark its passengers. Inside, there was a white marble entrance hall fringed by potted Rico Palms with busts of famous Austrians and Germans: Goethe, Beethoven, Bismarck, Martin Luther and such. That was as far as we got.

Marinda had come along with me as a witness and to take notes. She was wearing one of her shorter than short skirts today, and if she was dressed inappropriately, at least she looked spectacular.

Rolph came down the massive stairway in the front hall, wearing his ankle cuff, and Heinrich Wabstmann entered from the side with his body guard, Frau Liebshutz, who stared ferociously at Marinda. After exchanging stiff greetings, the five of us retired to one of the small parlors off the entrance hall that doubled as guest waiting rooms. Wabstmann looked put out, probably because he liked to be the last to arrive at any conference, but we were still waiting for Mr. Whittisack. There was nothing to do as we sat there but engage in small talk.

"Quite a concert last week," I mentioned. "It was a great way to end the season, and I'm sure the players, themselves, greatly appreciated that it was dedicated to Igor Bashenko. You could almost hear it by the way they were playing."

I thought I saw a slight frown beginning to press the corners of Wabstmann's mouth downward. He stood up and crossed the room looking out the window and then glancing down at his watch.

"Yes, it was a great show," he said, "but as for me, I can't tell what one symphony player is feeling by listening to an entire orchestra playing."

"Yes, I suppose that's right," I allowed, "as opposed to just listening to one person playing."

There was a hiatus of silence in the room, as Wabstmann looked at his watch again, obviously wondering where Whittisack was.

"I found it particularly sorrowful that Bashenko's previous "good friend," or maybe I should say, partner, Ida Dzygash, travelled all the way from Chicago to attend a concert dedicated to him," I said, trying to break the silence.

Wabstmann, immediately catching the sarcasm in my decision to use the same words the *Dispatch* had used under its picture of Ida and Janic Vadea, sneered at me. The atmosphere was going from bad to worse, and we hadn't even begun the conference yet. Wabstmann's presence was something I hadn't expected.

"So tell me," Wabstmann said, "on what subject do you intend to question Mr. Van Heyde today?"

"On the subject of Ida Dzygash," I answered, thinking there was no reason why either Wabstmann or Van Heyde would mind an inquiry about her, insofar as it related to the death of Igor Bashenko. In truth, I didn't know whether Wabstmann really even knew her, or of her, and if he did, it could only have been in connection with his nosing around the police station looking for reasons to fire Bashenko.

Wabstmann stood up abruptly. "Please excuse us for a moment," he said and he shepherded Van Hyde and Frau Liebshutz into an adjoining room containing a desk where they talked for close to five minutes. I could hear through the door that voices were being raised but I couldn't make out anything that was being said. Wabstmann and Ms. Liebshutz then returned, but Van Heyde lagged behind them at the desk for some reason. Then he too returned.

"Well, Gabe Whittisack isn't here, and it doesn't appear that he's coming," Wabstmann announced. Therefore, I'm afraid I'm going to have to terminate this conference. You'll understand, of course, Mr. Barchrist, being a lawyer yourself, I'm sure."

He then offered his hand to shake hands good-by, as did Frau Liebshutz. When Van Heyde shook my hand good-by, he deposited a small yellow sticky-note in it that he had probably picked up off the desk in the other room. When I got outside the walls of the Wabstmann castle, I glanced down at my palm.

The sticky-note said, "On the dam tonight—9:00 p.m."

"What do you suppose it means?" I asked Marinda.

"Didn't we cross over some kind of dam that creates this reservoir on our way out here?" she said. "I think it means he wants to meet you there at 9:00 tonight."

"Us—not me—us," I replied, "and we're not going to come alone. We're going to have my friend and client, Ron Herimus, lurking in the background for protection. I don't know how Van Hyde plans to get himself free enough to meet us there, but I guess we'll just have to go to find out."

Seemingly unconcerned about her safety, Marinda giggled. "Oh, Mr. Barchrist, I just want to say it's so exciting to work for you." Then she actually opened the car door for me as if I was somebody famous.

CHAPTER THIRTY SEVEN

There was no moon. It was pitch black, dark as a barn cellar. Ronnie drove the car halfway out onto the dam and slumped down in the seat to where he could not be seen from the outside because of the car's tinted windows. There were no lights. Nobody else was present. Beside Ronnie on the seat, was a Beretta semi-automatic .92F, a 9 millimeter Desert Storm Special and a Sig Sauer .551 ICS, also a semi-automatic.

Marinda and I stepped out of the car and walked approximately thirty steps away from it on the dam's walkway toward the eastern shore. We were 45 minutes early. On our left was a rock embankment made of boulders and other large rip rap rising approximately twenty feet above the quiet waters of the reservoir at about a fifteen percent grade. Twenty feet across the top of the dam on our right, was the top edge of the dam's cement wall rising 95 feet above the Big Walnut River at about an 80 degree grade. We couldn't see the water rushing through the spillway beneath us, but the sound it made was eerie and discomfiting.

At 8:50 p.m., a single flickering light appeared at the eastern extremity of the dam. It was Rolph Van Heyde. He had come on a bicycle—alone. After laying the bike in the grass, he approached us, walking along the dam with a flashlight.

"How did you manage to come alone?" I asked.

"Never mind that," he said. Pointing to his ankle bracelet, he added, "We only have a few minutes before this thing kicks in. So let's talk. I'll go first."

"Alright," I agreed.

"I didn't kill Bruge Biliuss," he began in a quiet voice. "I didn't kill Niels Blenker and I didn't kill Igor Bashenko. I can give you a lot of information about Ida Dzygash that you don't already know."

"Let's assume that's true," I replied, "how are you going to prove you didn't kill Bruge Biliuss or Igor Bashenko?"

"I'm not going to. You are," he said softly

He moved threateningly closer to me, touching my waist with his and looking straight into my eyes. I took a few steps back toward the right side of the dam, bringing myself closer to the railing protecting people from falling over the dam wall.

"I wasn't at Veteran's Memorial Hall when Biliuss died," Van Heyde continued.

"And how do we prove that?"

"You ask that Russian animal who drives his limousine for my cousin Heinrich to fess up and tell the truth about who he drove over to the Veteran's Hall on that day."

"Why? Why should I do that? He's already refused to give that information to anyone—to me, to the police, to anyone."

"I'm afraid we'll just have to leave the answer to that question for another time."

"And what about Niels Blenker?"

"That too," Van Heyde said impatiently. "Just leave that for another time too."

"And how do we prove you didn't kill Igor Bashenko?"

"I don't think I'm going to have to prove that, according to my lawyer. He thinks he can get the Interpol fingerprint excluded from evidence because it's so old and badly preserved. Look, you just get that Andropov character to tell the truth about who he took to Vet's Memorial on the morning of Biliuss's death and everything else will fall into place. I've got to go now. The police will be on me soon." He pointed to his ankle cuff.

"How do you suggest I get Picup Andropov to talk?" I asked.

"You'll find a way," he prognosticated, "and when you do, everything will fall into place."

"Maybe for you, but not for everyone else," I mumbled.

"What did you say?" His voice was raised now.

"I said maybe everything will fall into place for you if I can get Andropov to talk, but not for everybody else."

A look of rage seized his face, as he backed me up all the way to the railing with his chest and belly and began shoving my shoulders. I could feel the railing pressing into my back. I looked over the edge of the dam down toward the river 90 feet below, but I couldn't see it in the dark. I could hear the water rushing over the spillway. "Listen," he said. "Things may just fall into place for *you* right now if you don't do it. I'm an accused murderer because of *you*. How could you go to the police and tell them all those things to make me look like a murderer? What bad thing did I ever do to you?"

His hands and arms were tremendously strong. I could feel it as he lifted my 320 pounds off the ground. But I was getting angry too.

"Is this what you were going to do that day in the tower in Bruges with my Rosanne? Throw her off it?"

"No, but I could easily do it to you now, couldn't I? You could make a murderer of me yet, even though I am not a murderer."

I felt my feet dangling above the ground as he began pressing me over the railing. Marinda began screaming at him to stop. Then Ronnie turned the headlights from the car on and sprang out of the car holding his guns.

"Don't make me shoot, Mr. Van Heyde," he yelled, because I'll turn you into Swiss cheese with these."

Van Heyde was startled and for a moment he looked really confused. Then he dropped me to the ground and began running for his bicycle.

"Let him go, Ronnie," I said. "I think we got some information tonight that we're going to have to check out somehow, not the information we came to get, but nonetheless some important information."

"I'm completely confused," Marinda announced. "I know from your meeting the other day with his attorney that he's suspected of killing Biliuss, but I thought we came out here to get information about Ida Dzygash, that Wabstmann wasn't going to let him give us."

"Maybe we'll just have to take him at his word, and go see Picup Andropov again," I told her. "Better that things should fall into place for him than that I should fall over the dam. Thanks to you and Ronnie that didn't happen—tonight at least.

CHAPTER THIRTY EIGHT

There was only one person who hated Ida Dzygash more than Picup did. That was Anastasia Andropov. Both of their animosities stemmed from the same thing, Ida's effect on Igor and his good name.

Anastasia prefers *Nova Pravda* to the *Dispatch,* so she doesn't read the Columbus newspaper and she hadn't seen the picture of Ida and Janic Vadea in it. Nor did she know Ida was in town. Ani also hated Janic Vadea, because he had taken over when her father was relieved of his commission to direct the orchestra. She believed that Ida somehow had something to do with that, and that Janic definitely had something to do with it.

I used both of these things as leverage in taking my last shot at getting Picup to identify who his passenger was on the trip to Vet's Memorial the morning of the Bruge Biliuss murder. It was a complicated scheme, but I figured I would have to scare him somehow into talking. I did it by combining the truth with a white lie.

"Look Picup," I told him, "If Ani knew you were driving Ida and Janic Vadea around town together, who can tell how angry she would be at you? Who knows what she might do?"

"Why should she be upset? It's all by contract with Heinrich Wabstmann, under his Aiden Life Pharmaceuticals account."

I didn't let this reply stop me. Picup's revelation was interesting. So Wabstmann was expensing the transportation of Vadea and Ida around town as a business expense, but the Columbus Symphony Orchestra was not owned by Aiden Life Pharmaceuticals, nor did it do any business with Aiden Life. Was it Vadea who was doing business with Aiden Life?

"Tell me, Picup, except for when you drove out to the airport to pick up Igor Bashenko on that fateful day he didn't get off the plane, did Mr. Wabstmann ever ask you to drive Igor anywhere?"

"Never, and even on that day, that was, how would you say it, a donation from Ani and me to the Columbus Symphony. We weren't paid to go to the airport. We did it for free because it was Ani's father."

"Ah, so there may be a tax problem with you driving Ida and Janic around," I said. If there was, it would actually be Wabstmann's tax problem, but I didn't bother to tell Picup that. Besides, the IRS would never catch it.

I just wanted to scare him if I could into talking. "So, Ani will need to correct that by making a special separate personal or private charge to Wabstmann or something like that, and as your lawyer I will have to tell her you've been driving Ida and Janic around so she will do that," I said.

A sheepish look came over Picup, like he was ashamed of himself, maybe even scared. Although he hadn't said anything about it, it was obvious he had been driving the two of them around to more than just the Symphony Ball.

There were two things Picup was afraid of, Anastasia and the government, in that order. Then I played my ace. "Of course, as your lawyer, I could take care of this whole thing myself, without ever bringing Ani into it, but first you would have to tell me who it was that you drove to the Veteran's Memorial Hall on the day Bruge Biliuss died."

Picup began mumbling and pacing back and forth. "I could get in a lot of trouble if I told you that," he said.

"Picup, I know you're an honorable man, but it wouldn't be breaking any law to tell me."

"I'm not worried about the law," he said. "I'm worried about something else."

"What could that possibly be, Picup?"

He began pacing again. "Never mind about that, but you have to promise not to tell my wife I drove for Ida and Janic, and you can't tell anybody else what I'm about to tell you.

"Alright, Picup, who was it?"

"Janic Vadea."

I was floored, "Did you say Janic Vadea?" I asked in disbelief.

"Yes, Janic Vadea. So why is that so bad—because you were thinking I'd say Rolph Van Heyde?"

"Other than that and when he was with Ida Dzygash, have you ever driven Janic Vadea before?" I asked.

"No."

"But you picked him up at the Sheraton that morning—why the Sheraton? Was he staying there even though he had a condo here in Columbus?"

"I don't know. I don't know," Picup said. "All I know is that I dropped Mr. Van Heyde off at the Sheraton about 9:30 that morning and he told me to wait for him, but he never came back. About 10:00 a.m. Mr. Vadea came out of the hotel and told me to drive him to Vet's Memorial. He said Van Heyde had gotten sick or something, and he was going to make a delivery at Vet's for him. I drove him out to Vet's and he had me wait for him for almost two hours. Then we went back to the Sheraton; I dropped him off; and I left for the airport."

"But you had driven Mr. Van Heyde out to Whitehall earlier that morning, correct?"

"That isn't part of our deal, Winston, but yes."

"OK, Picup, you needn't worry about Anastasia finding out about your little secret. If she learns you were driving Janic and Ida around, it won't be from me."

Immediately, I left him and drove downtown to the Sheraton. A review of their guest registry for the date in question reveled that Vadea had indeed checked in the night before Biliuss was killed. I then drove to the police station. Shapiro and Picard wanted to haul Van Heyde in for more questioning about this, but I suggested that they get a copy of the hotel's guest registry and confront Vadea with it instead. Did he stay at the Sheraton that night and why?

I then accompanied them over to the Sheraton. As things turned out, the registry showed that Vadea had stayed there, not only on the night before Biliuss was murdered, but on many nights thereafter.

"Mr. Vadea checked in here a lot," a loose-mouthed clerk at the desk remarked, "sometimes with a woman."

"Was it always the same woman?" Picard asked.

"I don't remember," said the clerk. "Often, they came in later in the evening. She was a pretty good looking lady."

"Was this the woman?" Picard asked, showing the clerk the picture of Ida Dzygash that appeared in the newspaper.

"Maybe...I think so...but I can't really tell for sure from this," said the clerk.

CHAPTER THIRTY NINE

Gabe Whittisack's law office was a far cry from mine. We were both located in German Village, but that's where the similarities ceased. Whereas I was over a Dairy Mart, he was in a beautiful old tuck-pointed brick building in the center of the village. Whereas he had a dark, wood-paneled conference room with heavy velvet drapes and law books on the walls. I had no conference room, no paneled walls, no velvet drapes, no oak conference table and very few law books.

Gabe had agreed to produce Rolph in his office so I could ask him the questions Heinrich Wabstmann had stopped me from asking while we were in his home. Wabstmann was not present. There were no witnesses, just the two attorneys and Rolph.

"I followed your 'advice,' Mr. Van Heyde," I began. "I again asked Picup Andropov who he drove to Vet's Memorial on the morning Bruge Biliuss was murdered. This time he was more cooperative. He said it was Janic Vadea."

Whittisack began writing on a legal pad. A small satisfied smile began appearing around the corners of his lips. He looked up at his client, who released a sigh of relief and began smiling broadly.

"Sounds like I'm going to be free of any charges for the murder of Bruge Biliuss," Van Heyde announced.

"Not so fast, Mr. Van Heyde," I replied. At around 8:30 that morning, Picup Andropov dropped you off at the home of Ron Herimus. Why? What did you do there?"

Rolph was surprised by the question. "I...I went there to try to talk Mr. Herimus into using the anabolic steroid manufactured by Pharmae Bruxelles." Then he went silent.

"Why?"

"We were trying to sell it to all the competitors at the Schwarzenegger Classic."

"Who's 'we'?"

"The company—Pharmae Buxelles."

"Were you in Mr. Herimus' kitchen when you visited him?"

"I...I don't remember."

Then I got accusatory. "Look, Mr. Van Heyde, isn't it a fact that you *were* in Mr. Herimus' kitchen that morning; that while you were there you stole a syringe with insulin in it; and that syringe wound up at the scene of the murder of Bruge Biliuss?"

Van Heyde became very nervous, rubbing his huge hands together and blinking incessantly. As he answered, his voice showed he was clearly overwrought.

"I didn't kill Bruge Biliuss. Janic Vadea did. He killed Niels Blenker in Torhout too. He killed both of them using that little finger trick he plays with people's necks that he learned in the Serbian army when he was a captain in Kosovo. It's called *Lagano Ubija,* which means 'killing softly' in English. He stiffens his first three fingers; quickly drives them into the top of his victim's Adam's apple; and yanks downward."

Whittisack interrupted, "What motive could Janic Vadea possibly have to kill either one of those people?"

"Vadea's family was making a fortune licensing embryonic stem cell lines, developed at their research laboratory in the Balkans, to the Aiden Life Pharmaceutical Company for use in a drug Aiden was manufacturing called Ragasaline that it introduced on the market to cure Parkinson's disease. The use of these stem cell lines was a secret, unknown even to the FDA. A disclosure of that fact would have greatly injured the share price of Aiden Life on the New York Stock Exchange, because of the animosity conservatives and the Catholic Church hold toward abortion and the medical use of embryonic stem cells obtained from it. In fact, there was a question whether, if it were known stem cells were being used, such knowledge might even have led to a reversal of the FDA's approval of the new drug.

"Vadea himself owned 900,000 shares of Aiden Life, and he participated in the company's recent secondary offering to the tune of 200,000 more shares. So, you see, if it ever came out that Ragasaline was based on embryonic stem cells, the stock of Aiden Life would plummet and the Vadea family would lose its largest and most profitable laboratory contract.

"There were only a handful of people on the Aiden Life research team responsible for developing this drug who knew about the role of embryonic stem cells in the product. One of them was Bruge Biliuss. Another was Niels Blenker, and I forget who the others were. Each of these people was pledged to secrecy, but corporate learned that the secret was leaking out through Bruge Biliuss. So a plan was hatched to send him to America and get rid of him there."

"Who knew about this plan?" I asked.

Van Heyde looked morose, "Only my cousin Heinrich, Janic Vadea and myself, so far as I know. Yes, it's true I was originally part of the plan. I was to be the hit man, but I couldn't go through with it. On the morning that Biliuss was killed, I still didn't know exactly how I was going to accomplish it. I thought probably with my gun, using a silencer. As I told you, we were visiting all the competitors in the

Schwarzenegger competition, trying to get them to use our company's anabolic steroid. To set up an alibi, I had the limousine drive me out to the Herimus residence, so I could say I was busy selling Herimus on our drug at the time of the killing.

"Vadea was at the Sheraton with me, having checked in the night before. The plan was for him to follow the limo to the Herimus' residence, and I would tell the limo driver to go get some breakfast or coffee while he was waiting for me, thinking I was inside Herimus' house. But Vadea was then to drive me to Vet's Memorial where Biliuss would be getting ready for the competition, and then drive me back to Whitehall after I'd finished the job, and I would have the limo driver take me back to the Sheraton.

"While I was at Herimus's, I saw the insulin syringes lying on the towel there in the kitchen, and it occurred to me that I could dispatch Biliuss much more cleanly with one of those than with my gun. So I picked one up with my handkerchief and carefully put it in my pocket while Mr. Herimus was outside feeding his cat. Then, I got cold feet.

"I waited for the limo to return; got in it; and went back to the hotel with Vadea following. I told him I just couldn't do it; that I didn't have the financial motivation he and Heinrich had for doing such a thing; that I would do almost anything for Heinrich, but murder was out. Janic became enraged, telling me I could easily get away with it and get on the first plane back to Belgium. They'd never find me. I told him the same thing would be true if he did it himself and then went back to Serbia, but he screamed 'no, he had a career in music here to look after.' Then I gave him the syringe and said 'Well, here, you'll have to do it because I won't.' He took the syringe and left for Vet's Memorial in the limousine."

Whittisack looked exhausted from writing. "Can I get a copy of that?" I asked.

"No," he said. "I suppose my client has waived his privilege by telling me all this in front of you, even though you're a lawyer. But you're not *his* lawyer, and based on all of it, he's going to need a lawyer for the conspiracy charge when it surfaces, and I'm that lawyer. I'm sorry but I don't think it's in his interest, or mine, for me to give this to you."

"Well, can I ask him just a couple more questions then?" I said.

"Go ahead, but I may have to tell him not to answer."

"Mr. Van Heyde, you said Janic Vadea also killed Niels Blenker. How do you know this?"

"He told me. I told him I'd seen you and your girl friend having lunch with Blenker in Tourhout, and later he just told me that he'd gotten rid of Blenker too."

"While it makes sense" I said, "Blenker died of a broken hyoid that was snapped the same way Biliuss' hyoid was broken. But there was also something about a poisoned glass of milk in that case. I wonder what you know about that."

"Nothing."

"Well, I think we're just going to have to leave that one to the Belgian authorities anyway," Whittisack interrupted. "So why don't we just drop it here?"

"Ok, then," I said. "Then I have only one more area to cover with you. Tell me about your relationship with Ida Dzygash. Do you know her? Have you ever talked to her?"

Van Heyde sneered. "All I can say about that woman is that she's a bossy whore who drinks too much. She and Vadea were seeing each other almost the whole time Igor Bashenko was still maestro of the orchestra here. Bashenko didn't pay enough attention to her she claimed. She always said he wasn't enough for her. She also claimed Bashenko had lured her to Columbus with lies about the city and about their relationship. She hated him."

"So you knew her then?"

"Oh, yes. I even did her dirty work for her when I was in town. She would entertain Janic at the Bashenko condo, when Igor wasn't there, having me drive him over there in his car in the afternoon and drop him off so nobody would see his car parked there."

"Parked where?" I asked.

"At the Bashenko's condo," he replied. "Then around 10:30 or 11:00 at night, I'd come back with his car to pick him up."

"Did anyone ever see you who might be able to confirm this?"

"No. I'd always go to the back door, just ring the bell there and wait for it to open. Then we'd go down the steps and out the back way."

"Did you ever go into the condo itself?"

"Oh sure, many times, but just to wait there in the kitchen for Janic."

"Did Vadea have a key to the place?"

"Yes."

"Did you?"

"No."

CHAPTER FORTY

Gabe Whittisack didn't even wait out the day. He went straight to the police that afternoon with Van Heyde's story and took me with him to verify it. By 2:00 p.m. we were in Picard's office laying it all out for him. Picard was skeptical. Whittisack now had enough evidence to keep them from charging Van Heyde with the murder of Bruge Biliuss. There was the word of Picup Andropov that he'd driven Janic Vadea to Vet's Memorial on the morning of the murder; there was the evidence that Janic Vadea was staying at the Sheraton the night before; and, there was Van Hyde's testimony that he'd picked up the insulin syringe in Herimus's kitchen the morning of the murder and given it to Vadea back at the hotel. I asked if the charges against Ronnie were going to be dropped now, but Picard seemed to have already forgotten all about them.

"Oh, yah, yah," he said. "Conditions have changed completely. Your man will go free, but we're going slowly on charging anybody else right now. Van Hyde won't be charged on Biliuss's murder either. He was, however, clearly an accessory, and we can also charge him with conspiracy to commit murder if we want. We're going to see if we can get anything else out of him with his cooperation before we bring final charges against him for anything—kind of like plea bargaining in return for information. Besides, he's already been charged with one murder—Igor Bashenko's."

The evidence supporting this latter charge was pretty thin, I thought to myself. *But there was still no other suspect on the horizon.*

"We're going to watch Janic Vadea very closely for a while before we do anything more," Picard added.

I figured I'd done all I could for Ronnie Herimus, now, and that it was time to just leave the police to solve the Bashenko case on their own. The most I felt I could do for Igor's surviving relatives at this point was to win the lawsuit we had commenced on his behalf. So I "Noticed up" Heinrich Wabstmann for a deposition in the case. That may have led to a small explosion—literally. Three days after I received confirmation my Notice had been delivered, the Picup Andropov Car Service limousine blew up.

Foul play was more than suspected. There had definitely been a bomb. A very frightened Picup showed up at my office accusing me of being responsible, because I had supposedly let it be known he had revealed that it was Janic Vadea whom he drove to Vet's Memorial.

"That's ridiculous, Picup," I said, "Janic Vadea hasn't got the wherewithal to have your limo blown up, and, besides that, why would he want to? What good would it do him?"

"Well, we need to do something fast," Picup said, "because, otherwise I'm out of business. Maybe you should go ahead and settle the suit against Heinrich Wabstmann for pennies on the dollar so we can get another limo. After all, my late great father-in-law now has no use for the money the remainder of his contract is worth, and I'm sure he would be happy to see any proceeds from the suit you can get us go into providing another limo, so we can stay in business, and his daughter can continue eating." He frowned. "Although maybe I'm wrong about that."

Listening to Picup, I suddenly understood the meaning of the parting comments Van Heyde left us with at the Top Steakhouse when I turned down Wabstmann's offer to settle the case. Rolph had reminded us "Aiden Life was the biggest continuing client of the Picup Andropov Car Service;" that, "Picup Andropov hated his father-in-law;" and, that Igor's death, "brought an end to the embarrassment he had caused the Symphony board because now he'd never have to be re-employed."

It was hard to believe, but maybe the destruction of the Andropov's car occurred to make a settlement of the lawsuit at a much reduced amount necessary by putting Picup and Anastasia in a position where they now really needed money. Perhaps, my calling for Wabstmann's deposition had energized Wabstmann into having the limousine blown up. Would Heinrich Wabstmann do such a thing? Maybe—I couldn't help thinking about what Art Malone told me before the dinner I had with him and Heinrich at Lindy's. "Wabstmann is a man who would stop at nothing to get whatever he wanted."

A few days later, something else very strange happened. Ida Dzugash called me.

In a complete role reversal, she was now very forthcoming. "Darling, I really should apologize for the way I treated you when you came to visit me at my hotel. I had only been up for half an hour—with no coffee and no breakfast, and you know, these Marriott Residence Inns are comfortable, but not like home. I'm afraid I was too short with you."

"Well, what can I do for you, Ida?" I inquired.

"I understand you are going to take Heinrich Wabstmann's deposition soon, and that you've already deposed Janic Vadea."

I wondered how she knew that I had noticed Wabstmann for a deposition. "Yes, both those things are correct," I said, "although I may not have to depose Wabstmann if we can settle the case."

"You mean you *are* interested in settling the case? I thought all the negotiations on that were over."

Obviously, to know something like that, she had to have gotten the information either from Van Heyde, or from Wabstmann himself. My bet was that it came from Wabstmann because Van Heyde was under house arrest and probably *incommunicado* when it came to Ida. Vadea was only a minor player in the suit and unlikely to be privy to any settlement negotiations Heinrich Wabstmann was attempting. When I asked her where she got that information, she ignored my question.

"Well, Janic Vadea has asked me to call you. He says there's a little discrepancy at the end of his deposition, where you asked him if he knew me and he testified 'no.' Actually, the answer to that question should have been 'yes' and he wants to know if there's anything that can be done now to change that answer."

"Ida, he was given an opportunity to go over the deposition right after it was transcribed, and to note any changes he felt were necessary."

"Yes, darling, I know, but he didn't realize that your question related to the entire time period. He thought you were merely referring to the time period when Igor and I first came to Columbus together."

"While no, that's not what I was asking. I was asking if he ever knew you at any time. Have you read the deposition?"

"Yes I have. Obviously, he did meet me at some point, as the recent Columbus newspapers have shown."

I thought to myself, *Vadea had also refused to answer when I asked him if he had any business relationship with Wabstmann, other than as the Columbus Symphony conductor, but it was now clear that he did. At least, I remembered him refusing to answer, but maybe he had just lied and said "no," I couldn't remember for sure. Why was there such interest in correcting the record now? Perhaps Van Heyde told his Cousin Heinrich that he had pointed the finger at Vadea when he talked to Whittisack and me. There seemed to be a very strange relationship going on that involved Vadea, Wabstmann, Van Heyde and Ida Dzugash. I decided to go out on a limb by accusing her of things I really didn't know about.*

"Ida," I said, "I think it's time for you to fess up to the fact that you were seeing Janic Vadea quite regularly while Igor was the director of the Columbus Symphony. In fact, you even let him visit you at your condo when Igor wasn't there. Isn't that true?"

There was silence at the other end of the line.

"Did you give Janic a key to your place?"

More silence—

"Ida, tell me. Do you know anything about how Igor died?"

"Why would I know anything about that?"

"I don't know. Maybe it's because we all know now that Janic is a killer, and that he's murdered more than one person, and that the means of death he used in both cases matched—a piercing blow to the hyoid bone. We also now know that was also precisely the cause of death in Igor's case. You seem to have been Janic Vadea's girlfriend for quite a while. And now, for some reason, you seem interested in clearing up his testimony insofar as it concerns you."

"I didn't realize you hated me this much," she said.

"I don't hate you, Ida."

"But you're accusing me of—"

"Not accusing, asking."

"Well, it certainly feels like you're accusing me."
She became flustered, which was unlike Ida Dzygash."

"Ida," I continued, "why is it that you are calling on behalf of Janic Vadea? What's the real reason? He could have called himself, you know."

"I'm calling you because Janic is no longer here.

"What? Where is he?"

"He's out of the country. He went back to Serbia."

"Why?"

"I don't know. I think we should terminate this call now, Winston."

CHAPTER FORTY ONE

"Guess what! Serbia has no extradition treaty with the United States," Officer Shapiro announced as he entered Detective Picard's office. "After being shifted around and placed on hold by the Department of State for almost two hours, I've finished checking the matter out."

I was at the police station waiting to convert my statement concerning the strange phone call I received from Ida into writing, and Picard was pondering his next move. He felt that without more evidence he couldn't risk approaching Heinrich Wabstmann directly with the questions Van Heyde had raised about Wabstmann's relationship with Janic Vadea.

Rolph said his Cousin Heinrich knew about the murders of Biliuss and Blenker, and may even have had a hand in them, but Rolph's word was merely the word of a criminal conspirator, an accessory to murder. There was no corroboration. Vadea was needed for that, and he was gone. Picard was actually too afraid for his job to bother Wabstmann with the matter on the thin evidence he had. Heinrich Wabstmann was perhaps the richest and most powerful private personality in Columbus, and he would surely object to being asked questions about the nature of Ragasaline; the business dealings between Aiden Life Pharmaceuticals and the Vadea family laboratory; and the role of stem cells in Aiden Life's product. He would never admit that any employees of the company had been committed to secrecy about those issues.

Gabe Whittisack walked into the station in a huff, and began speaking to Picard very insistently. He suspected Vadea of Igor's murder because of the mode of killing that was used and the information that had recently come to light about his responsibility for the murders of Bruge Billiuss and Niels Blenker, where the means of death was exactly the same: a broken hyoid.

"You can't question Vadea about this since he's gone, and Van Heyde has already told us just about everything he knows. Now if you can't question Wabstmann about Vadea," he went on, "then perhaps you should get Ida Dzugash in here."

Shapiro and Picard thought that was a good idea. There was only one thing wrong. When they drove out to the Airport Marriott Residence Inn to see her, they discovered Ida had just checked out. Shapiro raced to the airport, asking me to meet him there to identify her if she was there, on the outside chance that her flight hadn't left yet, and Picard drove back downtown to see a judge about a warrant. As I was filling in the airport police with Ida's description, Picard was faxing the warrant to the airport administration. The warrant was for IATA computer records over the past two days on every flight out of Columbus. It showed that Ida Dzygash had purchased a ticket on Delta from Columbus International Airport to the John F. Kennedy Airport in New York, where she had a five hour layover, and from there, through to Paris, and on to Belgrade the next day. She was on her way to Serbia.

But she hadn't gotten very far along her itinerary yet. She was apprehended at the gate in Columbus and taken to an office upstairs at the top of the airport. It was a small room with metal walls, no windows, and a grey metal table in the middle. The lighting was fluorescent, and the seating was comprised of little more than card chairs. She flashed her black gypsy-like eyes at me as I entered the out of the way office, and I could see right then and there, the old Ida was back, scowling and mean. She was not happy. Gradually, the room filled with people: the Columbus police, the airport police, somebody from the airport administration, Shapiro and myself.

"What is all this for, Winston?" she snarled. "Is it because I dared to call you at your office to ask that Janic's deposition be changed? What do you want of me?"

Then Picard arrived.

"Going to Belgrade, are we?" he said. "Isn't that in Serbia? What for—vacation, or what?"

"Isn't that where your 'good friend' Janic Vadea lives?" I asked sarcastically.

"What do you want from me?" She was livid.

"Tell us, Ms. Dzygash, what is the nature of your relationship with Janic Vadea?" Picard began to bore in on her now.

"The nature of our relationship is we are friends. He likes music. I like music. We share a common interest in the Columbus Symphony Orchestra."

"Cook County Domestic Court records indicate you are divorcing your husband," I noted. "Is that because of your relationship with Janic Vadea?"

"That is none of your business."

"Well, what would you say," Picard retorted, "if we told you we had an eye witness to you and Janic carrying on together? Actually, we have more than one eye witness that you spent evenings with him at the Sheraton Hotel and in the condo you shared with Igor Bashenko."

"Are you in love with Vadea, Ida?" I asked. "The evidence we have isn't going to look very good in your divorce proceeding."

"What is the nature of your relationship with Heinrich Wabstmann?" Picard continued.

"Janic and Heinrich were friends," she replied, "and I became friendly with Heinrich through Janic."

Suddenly, she began breaking down. Tears came. This was a new Ida, one I'd never seen before. She looked distraught and her heavy make-up began to run. I looked down at her thin hands for some reason and noticed how long she wore her fingernails. The noise of a huge jet thrusting into the sky came from overhead. It was Ida's plane.

"Just friends?" Picard asked. "Did you ever hear any conversations between Vadea and Wabstmann?"

"Yes."

"And what were those conversations about? What do you know about Vadea's business with Wabstmann, or with Aiden Life Pharmaceuticals?"

"Am I under arrest?" she cried, "because if I am not, I'm leaving."

"You're not under arrest," Shapiro answered, "you are simply a person of interest. But I don't think you'll be going to Serbia today, because I think that was your plane we just heard."

"In relation to what crime am I a person of interest?" she demanded.

"The murder of Bruge Biliuss," he said.

"And, maybe the murder of Igor Bashenko," I added.

"How dare you," she shouted at me. "That's the second time you've accused me in Igor's case. What do you think, that I killed him?"

"Nobody thinks you did anything, Ms. Dzugash. You're just a person of interest to us because you might know some things that can help us solve these murders. It doesn't mean you're guilty of anything."

"That's right, Ida. For all we know, you're just running off to Belgrade after another one of your lovers, like you ran off to Columbus after Igor," I said dryly. Admittedly, I was trying to be biting. "But perhaps it would be better if you stayed out of Serbia and away from Janic Vadea for the time being," I suggested. "You know, he is under suspicion for the murder of Igor too. It's not just Rolph Van Heyde they suspect."

"That's ridiculous. Why would Janic want to kill Igor?"

"Janic might have wanted to do away with Igor because Janic hated Igor," I said. "You weren't there that day in the practice room when all the players in the orchestra rejected him as their maestro in favor of Igor, but I was. It enraged him. And ever since that day, Janic Vadea has never been able to get what Igor could get out of those musicians because they loved Igor and disrespected Janic."

"I know they had no respect for him, and it was killing him," she said tearfully. "And you—you helped Igor surmount him. You were there that day Janic had to turn the orchestra over to Igor." She was getting emotional. "But Janic did not hate Igor. I was the one who hated him. And now, with your permission, gentlemen, I'm going to continue along my way. There's another plane to New York in an hour, and if I get on it, I can still make my connection to Paris. So unless you want a suit against you for false arrest, I think you better let me leave."

One by one, the police filed out, leaving only Ida and me in the room. Suddenly, the hallway and everything around us became very quiet. As I was getting up to leave, she closed the door and looked at me with daggers in her eyes.

CHAPTER FORTY TWO

"You're getting too close, Winston," she said, "just too damn close."

"Close to what?" I asked.

"Too close to the truth, and I'm not going to let you mess everything up."

"Mess what up?"

"Everything," she said. "Janic and me, Janic and Heinrich, Janic's business, Janic's fortune, his reputation in the music community—you're just not going to mess it up."

"I don't understand what you mean," I said.

"I mean that everything was fine until you started snooping around trying to put together a defense for that friend of yours, Herimus, or whatever his name is. The police were ready to pin the murder of that Belgian weightlifter on him. Everything was fine until you sued Heinrich with that stupid claim for maliciously breaking Igor's contract to direct the Columbus Symphony. Janic's family business dealings with Heinrich were safe, and my Janic was again doing what he was put on this earth to do—make beautiful music. He loved being maestro of the orchestra, and he once again became its director. But you were about to spoil it all.

"You refer to him as Heinrich," I said. "Was Heinrich Wabstmann a friend of yours?"

"Yes, we became friends through Janic. You see, Janic and I became lovers shortly after you brought Igor and me here to Columbus so Igor could take over

Janic's job. Igor began to infuriate me. I was unhappy with the condo he rented for us in the Brewery District...too much noise and too many young tourists...and I wanted to live either in the Arena District or at Miranova Towers—you know, in a prime downtown condo high rise location. I became more and more miserable that I had ever agreed to leave Chicago.

"Plus, Anastasia hated me and I hated her and her boorish husband. They were stupid outdated communists. I was also receiving phone calls from a company called the Milo-Grogan Group, a detective agency hired by Joseph, who was certainly looking for me.

"And then Igor took up with that little whore violin player, Miriam Jaspers," she shrieked. "What right did she have to use up so much of his time, just because she's the symphony's concertmaster?"

"He went off almost every night with his violin to meet her?" With his VIOLIN! Why? What did he need the violin for? He was playing with her but he wouldn't make any music with me like we used to. And when I say he was playing with her, I don't mean playing only with his violin. She's a whore!"

"'No, no, Ida. You are so wrong,' he would whine. 'You are so beautiful, my dear. Why would I do such a thing? You are my one and only love.'"

"'I don't believe you, and you know what? I hate you,' I told him."

"So, Janic and I spent a lot of time together at Heinrich's mansion. It was there that I met another friend of Janic's, Rolph Van Heyde. I was very unhappy with Igor at the time, and when he'd go off to practice with the orchestra, or to meet with that little concertmaster slut, Miriam Jaspers, I'd go off to Wallendon with Janic. Janic knew how unhappy I was with Igor, and he hated Igor for that, almost as much as he hated him for taking his job.

"You remember when Igor was shot on stage at the Ohio Theater during the *1812 Overture*? That was Janic, shooting from the super structure above the concert shell. That's how angry he was at Igor for making a fool of him in front of the players in the orchestra practice room that day. You know. You were there. But Janic's shots didn't kill Igor—something about the larger the target, the larger the caliber you need to take it down, Janic later told me. He was only using a side-arm, left over from his days in the Serbian army.

"Later, we learned through Rolph that you were discovering too much on your little vacation to Bruges in Belgium—that Mr. Biliuss worked for a subsidiary of Heinrich's company; that he knew some very valuable research facts about the company's new product, Ragasaline; that there were stem cell lines involved in its manufacture; and, that company researchers may have been divulging this to you. We didn't know if you knew Janic's family company was supplying the stem cell lines, but Janic knew that if word ever got out that Ragasaline was made from stem cells, it would not only be the end of his family's business with Aiden Life Pharmaceuticals, but the end of the shareholder value for Aiden Life Pharmaceuticals, and Janic was a big shareholder in Aiden Life.

"When Rolph became too frightened to permanently shut Bruge Biliuss up about Aiden Life's company's secrets, Janic knew he would have to do it. He also silenced Niels Blenker when he learned you were talking to Blenker. 'Who cared if the world was minus two mouthy weight lifters?' he said. 'Look at all the lives Aiden Life was making better with its drug, Ragasaline.'"

All the time she was talking, she was circling around me, almost like a gypsy dancer trying to seduce her audience, and Ida could be very seductive. She was wearing six-inch heels and a gold, ankle bracelet, with a side-slit skirt that fell just above mid knee, and a colorful peasant blouse for a top, with a scarf to cover her neck. Her black hair was falling to her shoulders, much longer than most women of her age wore their hair, and her fingers were covered with rings. Closer and closer she came to me as she circled, staring into my eyes, enticing me with what she was saying. With nowhere to go, I tried to resist.

"And then, Janic finally did away with Igor," I said. "Was that at your bidding?"

"No, he didn't do that. I did," she whispered breathily, with a little trick Janic taught me that he learned in Kosovo, when they were cleansing away the Muslims." It's called *'Lagano Ubija'* in Serbian, or 'silent killing,' you know, like the song, *Killing Me Softly*.

Then she sprang at my throat, like a cobra uncoiling. I barely had time to see her three stiffened fingers coming at my neck before I felt her long sharp nails dig into me just above my Adams apple. I could feel her tearing at me, violently yanking downward with her fingers in my neck. She was going for my hyoid! Momentarily, I caught sight in my consciousness of what I thought were blood-spotted shaving abrasions on Igor's neck when I first saw his corpse in his bedroom. They were the result of Ida's finger nails earing at his throat. So it was Ida who killed him! She probably still had the key to their condo.

I tried to yell, but all that came out was croaking and gasping. Had she succeeded in snapping my hyoid? I rolled over on her and smashed a ham-like fist into her face. Some of the card chairs in the room clattered as they gave way to our bodies falling to the floor. Then I saw Ida get up and run out the door.

Suddenly, an airport policeman appeared. I couldn't speak, but I pointed out the door, and he got the idea. He took off after her, radioing for a medic for me on his shoulder radio as he ran. The police apprehended her at the gate to the next Delta flight to Kennedy International. They said she was in a very animated state of agitation, clawing at anyone who tried to touch her and screaming some word they didn't understand— "Janic! Janic!"

At Mount Carmel East Hospital, where I was taken from the airport, they performed a tracheostomy to restore my breathing ability. Ida had not succeeded in breaking my hyoid, they said, because of the size of my neck and all the excess fat. Being overweight had saved my life, but she did manage to create great but temporary damage to my breathing tube.

EPILOGUE

Ida Dzugash was tried for Murder One and Attempted Murder in the United States District Court for the Southern District of Ohio in Columbus. There was no death penalty specification because she co-operated with the United States Attorney's Office in providing information concerning a fraud perpetrated on the Food and Drug Administration by Aiden Life Pharmaceuticals. Today, she is serving back to back 30-year sentences for murder and attempted murder in the Federal Corrections Institution for Women at Aliceville, Alabama. Under the Sentencing Reform Act of 1987, she is not eligible for parole. Aliceville is a low security prison.

Columbus Police are still awaiting U.S. State Department Review of a proposed Extradition Treaty between the United States and the Republic of Serbia so that Janic Vadea can be brought back for trial. The treaty has been under review for five years. In the mean time, the Republic of Serbia has refused to extradite Vadea to Ohio for trial of the murder of Bruge Biliuss. Vadea and his family have exerted extreme pressure through the European Union organization, from which Serbia is currently withholding its membership application, to prevent the extradition of Vadea to Belgium where he can be tried for both the murder of Niels Blenker and Biliuss. The fact that the Vadeas are an old aristocratic family going back to the 1700's has not hurt.

Rolph T. K. Van Heyde pled guilty, on a plea bargain, in the United States Federal District Court, Southern District of Ohio at Columbus, to conspiracy to commit murder and to being an accessory to the murder of Bruge Biliuss. He was sentenced to nine years in the United States Penitentiary located at Marion, Illinois, with four years suspended. Van Heyde has become friends with me and Rosanne, and we visit him in Marion twice a year, once on his birthday and once around the holidays. Van Heyde has been very helpful in the investigation I have continued to conduct of Aiden Life Pharmaceuticals and Heinrich Wabstmann.

Sales of the drug Ragasaline have been temporarily halted in the United States by the Federal Food and Drug Administration while it undergoes a review of the process it used for initially licensing the sale of the product. The stock of Aiden Life Pharmaceutical traded downward so quickly when this was announced that trading was actually halted for a day. Since then, share price has continued to decline rapidly. The product is still being sold on the European market, but the number of stem cell lines Aiden purchases from the Vadea family has been radically reduced by more than half. Heinrich Wabstmann has been dropped from *Fortune Magazine*'s list of the 100 wealthiest individuals in the United States.

Anastasia and Picup Andropov are back in business with a new limousine purchased from the proceeds of the settlement of *Bashenko vs. Wabstmann, et al.* The settlement amount was greatly discounted because of Bashenko's untimely death and my refusal to share information concerning Biliuss's death with Heinrich Wabstmann, but mostly because of the overriding need for a new limousine placed on the Andropovs when their car exploded. The cause of the explosion was found to be a bomb, but it was never determined who placed the bomb.

My throat healed in time, but it took longer than expected. I now take every opportunity I can to point out to Rosanne that it was my pudginess that saved my life "when that succubus tried to claw me to death." If Rosanne complains about my over eating, I begin humming the tune, "Killing Me Softly."

With Rolph Van Heyde's help, I have commenced a "Qui Tam" action against Aiden Life Pharmaceuticals and its subsidiaries, alleging that the company promoted Ragasaline for uses not approved by the FDA; that the company failed to report key safety data regarding the product; that it failed to disclose the role embryonic stem cells played in the drug; that it was guilty of Medicaid fraud; and, that it paid illegal kickbacks to physicians. A Qui Tam action is a civil lawsuit, brought in behalf of the public's interest, by a private individual who has not necessarily been harmed by the defendant, to assist government prosecutors in the prosecution of a crime or the enforcement of federal regulations. The private individual who brings the suit is known as the "relator," and he brings the suit, under seal, on behalf of the United States, or some other governmental entity. Once the relator brings suit on behalf of the government, the Department of Justice, in conjunction with the U.S. Attorney have the opportunity to intervene in the suit, and to notify the defendant that the Qui Tam action has been filed. Settlement negotiations are currently going on in my Qui Tam action, somewhere in the range of three billion dollars, which will make it the largest Qui Tam settlement ever paid by a drug company.

Art Malone became the President of the Columbus Symphony Board after Heinrich Wabstmann was forced to resign because of the poor publicity he and Janic

Vadea received when Vadea absconded to Serbia. The press did an exposé on what seemed to be a very close friendship between the two men, but the articles left a lot of questions unanswered. Malone hired Jonathan Rainwater temporarily as visiting director of the orchestra for the next season. Rainwater is the first full-blooded Navajo to graduate from the Julliard School of Music.

ABOUT THE AUTHOR

 David Selcer authors the Buckeye Barrister mystery series, the first of which was DEADLY AUDIT, followed by DEAD BUT STILL TICKING. After graduating from Northwestern University, he attended Ohio State University Law School. He then had an exciting career practicing management labor law with a large national law firm for 35 years. Today, he lives with his wife for half the year in Sarasota, Florida, where he writes mysteries, and in Columbus, Ohio, the other half, which he still considers his home. He has five children and is an avid OSU Buckeye fan. He also continues to make employment case decisions for federal agencies on a part time basis as a Federal Agency Decision Writer.